Her
Executive
Protector

by

Sharon Saracino

This is a work of fiction. Names, characters, places, and incidents are either the product of the author's imagination or are used fictitiously, and any resemblance to actual persons living or dead, business establishments, events, or locales, is entirely coincidental.

Her Executive Protector

Cover Art by *Debbie Taylor*

The Wild Rose Press, Inc.
PO Box 708
Adams Basin, NY 14410-0708
Visit us at www.thewildrosepress.com

Publishing History
First Champagne Rose Edition, 2015
Print ISBN 978-1-5092-0348-2
Digital ISBN 978-1-5092-0349-9

Published in the United States of America

The pressure of Sam's fingers

increased slightly, and Maddie stepped closer. She saw the question in his eyes and didn't hesitate to raise her face to his. His breath feathered along her jaw before he covered her slightly parted lips with his own warm, firm ones. She melted against him, and the kiss deepened and evolved into something so much more than the brief offer of comfort Maddie suspected he'd intended it to be. She hesitated, her fingers curled tightly against his stomach, then surrendered to the riot of feelings the kiss evoked and allowed her hands to slide up the hard planes of his chest to twine around his neck. His arm circled her waist, and he pulled her more intimately against him. She felt the hard evidence of his desire pressing insistently against her stomach, and she was lost. She'd spent so many years carefully keeping people at a distance. For the first time in a long time, Sam Barstow made her want to let someone in. She wanted this man, and not just because he was trip over your own feet sexy. She wanted the whole package. She always had. She'd forced herself to forget because it hurt too much to remember. Considering her stay here was temporary, letting him back in might not be the best decision she'd ever make, but hell, she'd made worse.

Dedications

To my editor, Fran Sevilla.
Thank you for building me up, talking me down,
and being generally awesome at all the right moments.
~*~
Much gratitude to the tremendous twosome
D & S Buchbinder for your friendship and insight.
~*~
Endless love and appreciation to my Vinces,
who inspire me in ways they can't even imagine.
~*~
And, as always,
thank you to my readers for your love and support.
You make the magic happen.

Chapter One

Madigan awoke from a deep, dreamless sleep with a start, her heart pounding wildly. Disoriented, she jerked bolt upright. She cranked her head from left to right, puzzled by the dawn-lightened room for breathless minutes, until the events of the previous night came back to her. The forty-minute flight that turned into hours trapped on the tarmac, the toddler behind her using the back of her seat for kickboxing practice, the long, dark ride in the cab that ended in a place to which she'd never planned to return. She exhaled a sigh of relief as recognition struck. She was home. At least it used to be home. Glancing around, she realized the television screen was dark, though she distinctly remembered leaving it on after curling up on the sofa following her unsatisfying dinner of canned soup and crackers. Yet something had startled her awake. Something she couldn't quite…she slapped a hand to her mouth to stifle the gasp that threatened to escape as water gurgled in the kitchen sink. Someone was in the house!

She grabbed her cell phone off the coffee table and punched in 9-1-1 with shaking fingers, only to discover the phone was dead. In her fatigued stupor last night, she'd forgotten to plug it in. She dropped the useless piece of metal on the soft throw pillow. Slowly, soundlessly, Maddie carefully slid from the sofa and groped for the lamp. Holding her breath, she cautiously hefted it, gauging its weight. It would have to do. Quickly twisting the nut holding the shade in place, she tugged it free and set it on the floor at her feet, and then yanked the cord from the wall and wrapped it around the base. Figures she'd come home after all these years to be attacked and murdered by some crazed small town serial killer in the inherited home of her estranged father. She should have stayed in the city where the crazies all but wore signs. The faucet went silent and she heard the splash of water being poured, a muted click, and the rumble of a coffeemaker beginning to brew. A small town serial killer who felt comfortable enough in his victim's residence to break for a cup of Joe?

Putting one bare foot in front of the other, Madigan stealthily worked her way to the kitchen doorway praying there were no creaky boards in the newly refinished hardwood floor. A cabinet door snicked open, and she heard the ceramic clink of one cup against another. Heavy footsteps moved across the kitchen floor, and a chair screeched against the tile in protest as it was pulled out from the table. Whoever was out there made no attempt to be quiet and seemed to be making himself right at home. She clutched the lamp base tightly in her sweat slicked hand, barely able to maintain her grip. Maybe she should just creep to the front door and make a run for it? Sure, half undressed and nowhere to go. Not smart. though maybe the lesser of two evils? *No, damn it!* She thought. *This is my house!* Well, technically, anyway.

Pulse racing, it felt as though a flock of butterflies had decided to hold a spontaneous convention in her stomach. She knew her anxious breathing must be audible and thanked her lucky stars for the noisy gurgle of the coffeemaker. Flattening herself against the wall, she closed her eyes briefly and bit her lip, before carefully peeking through the doorway. A set of very broad shoulders encased in a tight, sweat-stained T-shirt was the first thing she noticed. A man sat at the table with his back to her, scribbling on a legal pad, wearing a red bandana tied around his head like a headband, and his long legs encased in torn jeans. A cell phone, a set of keys, and a pair of mirrored aviators were carelessly tossed on the table. A worn leather tool belt lay on the floor near his feet. Madigan had read about gangs of thieves who broke into older homes to steal the copper pipes for drug money. Gangs! Hadn't she just seen that story on the news about gangs moving into small town America to peddle their drugs? Was he wearing gang colors? Well dammit, whoever he was, he wasn't getting his hands on *her* pipes!

She made it almost halfway across the kitchen on her rubber legs before some instinct alerted him to her presence, and the chair slid back as he turned in her direction.

"Don't move," Madigan warned in a voice she intended to be strong and forceful. Unfortunately it came out a nervous, breathless whisper.

"What the hell...?" he grumbled, almost completely turning toward her and rising out of the chair.

"Get the hell out of my house," she shrieked bringing her arm up and swinging the heavy lamp right at his head with all of her strength. Madigan belatedly realized the wide, blue eyes were set into one of the most shocked, familiar, and incredibly attractive faces she'd ever seen.

****

Sam Barstow's head exploded. At least it felt that way as the lamp caught him right above the ear, knocking his bandana flying and sending him heavily to his knees. He swore he actually felt his skin splitting. His eyes clamped shut against the pain, leaving him temporarily blinded. He planted his hands on the cool tile, concentrating on his breathing, while hoping she didn't decide to take another shot at the back of his head while he was down.

Thankfully, he heard his assailant move away, and detected the muted beeps of his cell phone. Her voice was low and husky and took him right back to fast cars and warm summer nights. His groin twitched in involuntary response. The bitch had hit him with a brass lamp, and he was fantasizing about her? It was official. He'd lost his mind. Maybe he needed to get out more. He had to be nearing the point of desperation if he was getting aroused by a sleep rumpled woman who ranked high on his shit list.

He heard the phone click off and the rattle of his tool belt. If she'd nearly taken him out with an old lamp, she'd be a hell of a lot more lethal with his claw hammer. He'd only had a brief glimpse of her before he couldn't see anything at all, so it was difficult to tell how much she might have changed. Well, he'd deal with that in a minute, as soon as he managed to uncross his eyes.

Climbing slowly to his feet, assisted by the back of the chair, he blinked rapidly and groaned as he turned to face his would-be attacker. Yep, as small and slender as ever, her shapely bare legs poked out of a baggy pair of plaid boxers riding low on her narrow hips. A white tank top hugged her curves, and he could detect a hint of dusky nipple through the thin, clingy cotton. Her thick, dark hair was flat on one side, a riot of tangled curls on the other, and her green eyes were wide and wary as she braced her bare feet shoulder width apart, brandishing his hammer in front of her with two trembling hands.

"Just stay right over there." She waved the hammer threateningly in the air. "The police will be here any minute, so don't even think of trying anything."

"Nice to see you again too, Madigan," he wheezed dryly, annoyed that his voice lacked its usual authoritative tone. Her brows sailed into her hairline, and she lowered the hammer a fraction of an inch. "Welcome home."

"Sam?" she whispered, the fear and uncertainty clear in her voice. "Oh my God, it *is* you. Sam Barstow, what in the hell are you doing here?"

"I'm here to finish the roof. Didn't mean to scare you. Dawson told me you weren't coming till next week. If I knew you were here, I would have knocked. Hell!" His laugh came out more like a rusty croak. "If I knew I was going to take a crack in the head, I probably would have stayed in bed."

Sam heard a car door slam and realized Pine Grove's finest had already arrived. Well, why the hell not? It was a quiet town, and they didn't have a lot to do on a Saturday morning. He sighed. Whoever was on duty would make sure he never lived this down. Madigan jumped as a brisk knock sounded at the front door. She inched carefully past him, still gripping the hammer.

She'd always been pretty, but over the years Madigan Moran had matured into a real stunner. Too bad there was a heart of stone beneath those lovely breasts. He knew it better than anyone.

"So, what? A dead man's work order gives you free rein of the place?"

"Already told you. Didn't know you were here."

"You just stay put," Maddie directed over her shoulder as she scooted to the front door and threw it open. Sam heard voices and cringed. Bill Jessup. Oh yeah, he was going to be on the receiving end of some serious ribbing. Then again, he supposed it *was* kind of funny. Or at least it would be once the bleeding checked and his head stopped pounding like a runaway jackhammer.

"Sam." He heard the familiar voice of his friend dripping with amusement.

"Bill." He turned toward the man and avoided the outstretched hand.

"Miss Moran reported someone broke into her house to steal her copper pipes." The officer smirked.

"I see. Very astute of her to figure that out. Well, looks like you've caught me red-handed." He held out his hands in front of him. "You wanna cuff me, officer?"

"Red-handed and red faced too, by the look of it." Bill laughed. "Did it ever occur to you to knock?"

"Why would it? I didn't know she was here. Had the day free, figured it was a good chance to get some work done."

"Gonna get pretty hot up there today," the officer observed. "Might want to finish before noon. 'Course I guess you might have to wrestle her for your hammer first. Think you're up to it?"

"You're a funny, funny guy, Bill. Now do you think you can vouch for my sterling reputation to the lady and let me get to work?" Sam growled. He noticed Madigan's arms had dropped to her sides, but her fingers still clutched his hammer in a white knuckled grip as her eyes bounced nervously from one of them to the other.

The policeman turned back to Madigan with an encouraging smile.

"While I don't have the time or the mental capacity to remember all of Sam's vices, Miss Moran"—he laughed—"I can promise you breaking and entering, theft of old plumbing fixtures, and ravishing unsuspecting women aren't among them. Sam and your dad were good friends, and Sam's done most of the work on this place. I think this has just been a big misunderstanding."

"Not exactly the glowing endorsement I was hoping for," Sam replied.

"Sure you don't want to go down to the hospital and get checked out?" Bill frowned. "You're bleeding pretty good there, buddy. Might need a couple of stitches."

"Nah, I'll be fine. Head wounds always bleed like a bitch. Had worse." Sam waved him off and grabbed a kitchen towel from the drawer, folding it into a thick square and pressing it to his scalp.

"Okay, but if you have even the slightest hint of concussion, you get your ass down there, understand?"

"Yes, Mother," Sam mumbled. "Are we done?"

"Yep." Bill raised a hand to slap him on the

shoulder, then pulled back, obviously thinking better of it at the last minute. "Nice to meet you, Miss Moran. I'll let myself out."

Madigan jumped, seeming to come out of a trance when the policeman spoke to her directly. She offered her hand then realized she still had a death grip on his hammer. Her cheeks colored attractively as she quickly set it on the table and turned to take the officer's outstretched palm.

"Thank you, officer. I'm sorry to have wasted your time."

"Not at all, and please call me Bill. Glad it was just a mix-up." He squeezed her hand.

"Thanks again for coming."

"Anytime." Bill smiled. "See you, Barstow."

Sam nodded shortly, wincing as the movement caused the pounding in his head to ratchet up a notch. The policeman smirked knowingly before striding across the parlor and out the front door leaving an uncomfortable silence in his wake.

****

Madigan risked a glance at Sam Barstow where he leaned against the kitchen counter with the towel plastered to his head. He'd always been attractive, even as a teenager, but he'd grown even more so over the years. Broad shoulders and a heavily muscled chest tapered to a narrow waist, flat stomach, and slim hips encased in snug denim. The jeans clung to his strong thighs and continued down over long legs terminating in a dusty pair of steel-toed work boots. He wore his dark hair short, almost military style, which only emphasized his long, corded neck and chiseled jaw. Though closed at the moment, his eyes were still a shocking blue, crinkled at the corners, and set in a tanned, slightly lined face that hinted at a good deal of time spent outdoors.

All in all, Sam Barstow presented quite an attractive package, and Maddie was annoyed to feel a warm tendril of desire curl low in her stomach. Which she pointedly ignored. Sam Barstow had been just the first in a long line of bad decisions. Predictably, her latest relationship had ended disastrously too, so much so she'd jumped at the opportunity to get out of town for a while. Ian Sutherland was a lying, cheating snake, and yet poor choices in men seemed to be pretty much the status quo in Maddie-world. She sure as hell wasn't looking to revisit past mistakes. In fact, she wasn't looking. Period.

"Um, why don't you come and sit down over here." Maddie frowned at the timidity she heard in her own voice.

Sam held the towel to his head with one hand and staggered his way across the kitchen until he felt the back of the chair, then fell into it heavily.

"Yeah, sorry about the towel," he rasped. "I'll replace it."

"Oh, uh, I hardly think that's necessary. I mean, I caused the bleeding, after all. Of course, if we're going to be technical, it's your fault for scaring the hell out of me." With no idea what else to do, she filled a glass of water from the tap and set it on the table in front of him, then ducked into the small, recently renovated bathroom off the kitchen to grab a bottle of aspirin.

She shook a couple of tablets from the bottle and set them next to the water, then watched as he carefully felt the surface of the table, keeping his eyes closed, until his hand encountered the glass. He picked it up and raised it to his full, well-formed lips. Maddie felt the heat staining her face when his eyes suddenly snapped open, and she realized she'd been caught staring, mesmerized by the way his throat worked as he chugged the liquid.

"I'm sorry." Maddie backed away from the piercing gaze. "I didn't realize I could actually do so much damage with that old lamp, but...well, it never entered my mind it would be you, and a girl can't be too cautious, you know." She trailed off.

"This wasn't exactly the way I'd planned to start the day," Sam replied hoarsely.

"Look, I told you I was sorry—"

"Hey, you woke up to a strange man in the house, acted first, and asked questions later. Can't blame you. Frank would be proud to know he raised such a smart, self-sufficient daughter."

Madigan stiffened and turned away. "Frank can't take credit for anything about me. In fact, as you may recall, from the time I was ten, I pretty much raised myself. Glad to hear you think I did such a great job."

Maddie left him sitting in the chair, snagged another towel from the drawer, and spread it on the counter near the refrigerator. Yanking open the freezer, she emptied an ice cube tray onto the cloth and wrapped it into a small bundle, carefully keeping her back to him. She'd become a strong, independent woman in spite of her father, not because of him, right?

"Here, I'll get that." Maddie heard the chair scrape back and felt Sam come to stand behind her.

"Done," she announced briskly. She turned and nearly bumped her nose on his chest. She automatically took a step back and smoothed a hand down the front of her tank. "Sorry, I didn't realize you were standing so close. You caught me off guard."

"Seems it's becoming a habit," he replied in a wry tone. He tossed the bloodied towel into the sink, took the ice pack from her, and pressed it to his scalp with a grimace. "Listen, I know your dad's a sore spot for you. I guess we had very different relationships with him."

"If by that you mean you apparently had one and I didn't, then yeah, you're right."

When she'd needed a father, he hadn't been there. When he finally remembered he had a daughter, she no longer needed him. After years of silence and a twelve-step program, he'd turned up on her doorstep six months ago, an unexpected stranger seeking a relationship and absolution. And now he was dead. He hadn't been a regular part of her life in years, so why this sudden rush of sorrow? The throat-tightening grief was a startling and unexpected emotion sucking at her like the undertow after a storm at the Jersey shore. It didn't make sense. She swallowed hard over the thick knot, angry at the fact her father still had the power to make her feel anything at all. Maddie crossed her arms over her chest when she noticed Sam's eyes had wandered there more than once. It belatedly occurred to her she was half dressed.

"I just wasn't thinking," he continued. "Can you help me get this shirt off? It's covered with blood."

"You expect me to believe you can't undress yourself?" Maddie doubtfully eyed him, relieved she didn't have to deal with any more of her conflicted emotions regarding her father for the moment. "You may be all grown up, Sam Barstow, but your pick-up lines haven't improved much."

Sam's laughter was warm and far too intimate for Maddie's fragile peace of mind. She took another step back, just to be safe.

"Maybe if I was interested in picking you up, I'd try a little harder. Fact is, the bleeding is starting to slow down, and I don't want to disturb it. The shirt's beyond salvageable anyway, so if you can help me stretch the neck out to get it over my head, I can keep the ice in place."

"Oh." Maddie ducked her head and stepped behind him, relieved he couldn't see her burning cheeks. She'd just cracked him with a lamp and had been fully prepared to bash him in the head with a hammer. Now she was disappointed to discover he wasn't trying to flirt with her? She must be one screwed-up chick. Maybe she should reconsider therapy after all. She refused to analyze why she trembled enough to make it nearly impossible to get her fingers into the neck of his tee and gather it together and away from his head, but finally she managed to get a good grip and started to tug.

"Are you sure?" she asked hesitantly. "It's probably easier to cut it off, but it seems a shame to ruin it…I mean, maybe the blood will wash out?"

"It's a T-shirt, Maddie. Hardly irreplaceable."

"Oh, that's right, I forgot! Money is no object to the high and mighty Barstows."

"That's not what I meant, and you know it," he replied. "You know me better than that. At least you used to."

"I thought I did…whatever. In my opinion, you're either very trusting or very foolish to turn your back on a woman who just attacked you."

"Maybe. But I figure I'm safe from the Wrath of Moran since the cops have verified my respectability."

"I don't recall him verifying anything other than the fact that you weren't a thief or inclined to violence toward women. That doesn't make your respectability a foregone conclusion." Maddie fumbled in the cutlery drawer until her fingers closed around a serrated steak knife. Sawing at the hem, she cut through the material, and set the knife on the counter. Then she gripped the frayed edges and yanked until the tear reached the neck. Maddie picked up the knife again and sliced through the remaining band of fabric. "There."

Sam used his free hand to pull the shirt the rest of the way off without further comment, while Maddie struggled to tear her gaze away from the tempting sight of his smooth, tanned, and touchable skin. Wadding the ruined shirt into a ball, he deposited it in the trash near the back door.

"Thanks."

Maddie tried not to stare at the tempting expanse of exposed chest as Sam turned back to where she remained frozen near the sink. She failed. Averting her eyes when he caught her staring again, she busied herself with pouring a cup of coffee from the all but forgotten pot. She clutched the mug to disguise the fact her hands were shaking. Waking up in a strange house to find a strange man in the kitchen would have that effect on anyone, right? It had absolutely nothing to do with the fact that the strange man was Sam Barstow or the appealing package of rippling muscles now exposed to her view. Nope, nothing at all.

"Didn't bring any milk since I don't use it, but

there's a sugar bowl in the second cabinet on the left," he offered as he repositioned the ice pack with a grunt.

"I take it black, thanks. You seem to know right where everything is," she remarked, surprised at the sullen tone she heard in her voice. It made her sound as though she resented the fact that he knew more about her father than she did. Which, of course, was ridiculous. She hadn't wanted to know.

He shrugged. "Spent a lot of time here."

"Why?"

"Why?" His voice told Maddie he was genuinely puzzled at her question. "Look, Madigan, I know you had your issues with your father, and I guess I understand why, but I always liked Frank, and he was a good friend when I needed one. Now, I'll leave you to get on with your day. I promised I'd get this house finished for you, and I mean what I say. It shouldn't take long, but I'd better get to work."

"For me? What do you mean for me?" Maddie persisted, even though it was clear from Sam's sudden jerky movements he felt he'd shared too much and had become uncomfortable with the conversation. "And as for my having issues with my father, he knew where I was for years. Maybe he should have made an effort a little earlier."

"Maybe. Or maybe since you were the one who walked away, he anticipated the reception he was likely to receive and wanted to save himself the disappointment. Not my call. I'll run upstairs and borrow one of Frank's T-shirts if you don't mind," he said, changing the subject. "It's gonna be hot on that roof today, and I don't need a sunburn adding insult to injury. The clothes still boxed in his room?"

"I have no idea. I haven't been upstairs," Maddie said, her mind whirling. Sam moved toward the stairs and she was right behind him.

"Why not?" He frowned. "Your room was ready. Where did you sleep?"

"On the sofa." When she'd arrive late last night, the outside of the house appeared completely unchanged. The same could not be said for the totally renovated interior. She didn't realize she'd been both dreading and craving some feeling of familiarity until she stepped inside and discovered it wasn't forthcoming. It was equally surprising and uncomfortable. Feeling restless and unsettled, she'd been too tired to sort out whatever emotional upheaval she might experience upon seeing her old room. She figured she'd be better prepared after a good night's sleep.

Instinctively Maddie grabbed for the belt-loop at Sam's lower back to stop him from continuing up the stairs. Her fingers tingled as they inadvertently brushed the skin of his lower back. It was as silky and warm as she remembered. Judging by his swiftly indrawn breath, he'd felt the same awareness. She jerked her hand away and gripped it hard in her other one.

"What did you mean when you said you promised you'd finish the house for *me*?"

Maddie sensed more than heard Sam's deep sigh. Slowly he turned and regarded her from the second step. His mouth compressed in a thin line, and his brows drew together in a deep frown. It was clear he weighed his response.

"Frank and I have been working on this house for over a year. He knew he was on borrowed time, and he wanted to leave you something secure. He poured every penny he had into making this place somewhere you'd be proud to call home. He didn't want you to have to struggle anymore."

"He didn't want me to struggle? That's rich!"

Maddie's eyes filled with a quick rush of tears. She wasn't sure if they were the result of the anger she wore like a shield against her father, or this new tug of grief and regret she'd felt like a dull, unwelcome ache in her chest ever since Dawson appeared at her door and announced her father was gone. And the completely unexpected appearance of Sam Barstow the minute she opened her eyes wasn't doing a whole lot for her emotional equilibrium, either. He was the last person she'd expected to run into on this little trip down memory lane. In any event, the tears came out of nowhere and took her by surprise. Her insides churned like they'd been dumped in a food processor and set on liquefy. She should never have come. She thought she'd successfully written her past out of her heart years ago. Now she was having that certainty challenged at every turn.

"Maybe he should have worried about that a little sooner. Like maybe before he became a drunk and let the bottom of a bottle become more important to him than his family, or maybe when my mother died and I was left to handle things no kid should even have to know about. Or maybe when I finally got out and tried to make a life and my father never bothered to see if I was dead or alive until six months ago. That? *That* was a struggle. My life now is a cakewalk in comparison."

"You didn't have to run away to save yourself, Maddie. You had me," Sam snapped in a hard voice, shocking the hell out of her. She blinked away another rush of tears as she stared at him, but he didn't look away, just continued to regard her with a cold, curious expression as though she was a puzzle he couldn't quite put together. She swallowed hard and lowered her gaze.

"Maybe it wasn't myself I was worried about saving."

She moved stiffly over to the sofa and snagged her overnight bag from the floor where she'd dropped it the night before. On her way to the bathroom, she paused and settled her gaze on Sam who remained frozen in place watching her.

"Anyway, thank you. It's a lovely house. You and Frank did a wonderful job. It would be any girl's dream. But fresh paint and granite countertops aren't quite the same thing as having a father when you need one. I always had a roof over my head, but I would have happily lived in a cardboard box if it meant I had a father for whom I was a priority, rather than an option. Still, all your hard work will pay off. It'll make the house much easier to sell."

She stomped past him and through the kitchen to the bathroom, slamming the door firmly behind her.

Chapter Two

Madigan felt marginally more human and slightly less shrewish after a long, hot shower. She pulled a clean pair of jeans and a simple yellow tee over her incongruently feminine bra and panties. She'd expected to spend her time in casual clothes sorting through a disaster area and had packed accordingly, but it didn't mean she couldn't indulge her fondness for decadent lingerie. As far as she was concerned, there was simply no excuse for ugly undies, no matter what a girl might be forced to wear over them. She didn't bother with make-up, though she did take the time to blow dry her now clean and unruly curls into soft waves that fell past her shoulders, and then she brushed them back into a loose ponytail. She'd expected her father to be living in squalor. That's how alcoholics lived, right? Just one more preconceived notion about her father, and the life she imagined him living, shot to hell. When he came to see her, he claimed he'd been sober for nearly nine years. She hadn't believed him. Or maybe she'd been afraid to. She shouldn't feel guilty about doubting him, he'd let her down before. And then he died and left her everything like she'd been someone important to him. Instead of making her feel better, it only made her feel worse.

She stuffed her nightclothes into her bag, then took it and dropped it on the small landing at the foot of the stairs. Sam had apparently taken her large bag up to *her room* already as it was nowhere in sight. She supposed she had to climb those stairs, sooner or later, but at the moment, later looked better than sooner. And besides, right now she owed Sam Barstow an apology. Not for the lamp to the head. That was self-defense after all, though in hindsight she did feel bad about it. No, she owed him an apology for shrieking at him like a fishwife and taking her hurt and resentment about her father out on him. Her father had finally reached out a hand to her, and she'd slapped it away. She drew in and blew out a deep, painful breath. It was the first time she admitted to herself the ball had been left in her court, and she'd stood there dribbling, lacking the courage to actually to take the shot. At any rate, nowhere in the whole equation did the blame lie at Sam Barstow's feet, and she needed to stop acting like a petulant child.

She heard the dull, rhythmic thud of his hammer overhead. Maddie couldn't believe he'd actually stayed and climbed the steeply angled roof and gone to work while sporting a lump the size of a goose egg on his head. Most men would have told her to get screwed and gone home. She was a fair cook. Maybe she could make a peace offering of lunch if she had something besides a granola bar, a sleeve of saltines, and assorted condiments to work with. Besides, if she stayed for a while, she'd need to get a few groceries anyway. There should be a store within walking distance, but it wouldn't be much fun hauling the bags home all by herself. She heaved a heavy sigh. She quite possibly was going to have to ask Sam for a favor. And he sure as hell didn't owe her one. In fact, all things considered, she might actually have to beg. She retrieved her phone from between the couch cushions, plugged it in to charge, and then grabbed a bottle of cold water from the fridge and stepped outside to eat crow.

Sam's ladder stood propped against the house right next to the back door.

"Sam?" she called out.

His sweat slicked face appeared over the edge of the roof. The mirrored sunglasses hid his eyes so she couldn't read his expression. Maddie waved the bottled water enticingly in the air. Unbelievably he smiled, as though she hadn't attacked him, acted like a thwarted child, and stomped away in a temper. Of course, he was probably just dying of thirst.

"Couple more nails and I'm done. Be right down," he called back.

Shading her eyes against the sun with the palm of her hand, Maddie surveyed the small backyard. A wooden privacy fence lined with mulched beds interspersed with pops of color from blooming crocus, hyacinths, and tulips surrounded the whole area. A flagstone path led to a small gazebo standing in the shade of a sturdy oak. Bright blue jays flitted among the branches, announcing their presence with loud, discordant squawks. Lilac bushes surrounded the gazebo. A Victorian bird feeder mounted on a tall metal post stood in the back corner. The scene distorted through a film of tears, and Maddie's lungs felt suddenly too tight to draw in air. She knew this place, knew it well. Except for the absence of a swing set and a blow-up wading pool, it was the backyard she remembered before it had become neglected and gone to ruin. The backyard from her childhood. When she'd still had a family. When they'd still been happy.

"Oh God," Maddie whispered under her breath as the bottle of water slipped from her nerveless fingers and rolled into the grass. Her throat tightened to the point of pain, and she took deep, gasping breaths that did nothing to quiet the roiling nausea that suddenly erupted. She began to shake. A random, full-body trembling buckled her knees, and would have sent her to the ground if Sam's strong arms hadn't suddenly caught her.

"What's wrong?" Sam's voice penetrated Maddie's jumbled thoughts.

"The yard," she forced out through tightly clenched teeth. "It's…it's…"

"Is there something wrong with it?"

"No, it's perfect. Perfect." Despite her best efforts, the sobs clawed their way up from her chest, squeezing her heart in a tight fist along the way. "It's perfect…damn."

She knew Sam had no idea what had triggered her tears, and she couldn't seem to stop crying long enough to explain. On some level she realized her reaction was silly, unreasonable, and completely out of proportion, but it didn't seem to matter. Sam finally hooked an arm beneath her knees and swung her against him. He kicked open the back door and carried her through into the parlor where he lowered himself onto the couch keeping her on his lap as she fisted her hands in the front of his shirt and continued to weep. She burrowed her face into the warmth of his solid chest, comforted by the familiar and long-forgotten scents of cotton, sweat, and sunshine. He let her cry until her sobs subsided to sad little hiccoughs. Finally, she drew in a long, shuddering breath and pushed away from his chest.

"Well, this is awkward. Would you believe I actually came out to apologize for my earlier behavior? I even intended to offer you lunch, provided you could haul my ass to a store. I promise I wasn't intending to have a meltdown…which now probably necessitates another apology." She sighed.

"Forget the apology." Sam's expression was puzzled. "But maybe you could clue me in as to what set you off? I'd like to avoid a repeat performance."

Maddie drew in another deep breath and slowly blew it out. She climbed out of Sam's lap and moved to the armchair sitting at a ninety-degree angle to the couch. Still close enough to touch though, she realized, as her leg came to rest against his.

Now that she'd regained some measure of control, she felt like an idiot for letting herself cuddle in his lap like a child needing comfort. Although for a minute it's exactly what she'd felt like and unbelievably, he'd stepped up to the plate.

"I guess you're *really* wishing you stayed in bed this morning about now, huh?" As a rule, Maddie didn't do tears. She figured she'd cried all the tears she'd ever been born with years ago. Yet, in less than twenty-four hours, she'd turned into a leaking, sniveling pile of goo. She didn't like it much and couldn't believe she'd lost complete control of herself like that, and in front of Sam Barstow, of all people. A grown up Sam Barstow who was hot as hell, to boot. Well, it hardly mattered how attractive he was. For one thing, a man was the last thing she'd come here for and for another, she'd pretty much ensured any feelings he might have ever had for her were as dead as disco. She'd thrown away her first class ticket and jumped off that ship years ago without a life preserver and without a good-bye. At the time, it seemed the only choice. Clearly, he'd been informed she was coming but didn't expect her until next week. No doubt that was the reason he'd planned to finish the work today. He hadn't wanted to run into her any more than she'd expected to see him.

"What? And miss all this excitement? Pine Grove is a small town. I take my cheap thrills where I can find them." His lips curled, and Maddie noticed he still had a dimple in his left cheek, partly hidden by the faint shadow of dark stubble along his lower face and jaw.

"I hardly think lamps to the head and semi-hysterical women constitute thrills, cheap or otherwise." She returned the grin.

"Hey, you have your idea of thrills and I have mine. Now spill. What set off the waterworks?"

Maddie found her chest didn't feel quite so tight now. Sam had always been remarkably easy to talk to, easier by far than the therapist she'd been to years ago who nodded sagely and periodically glanced at his watch, always reminding her he was being paid to listen.

"Memory ghosts," Maddie sighed.

"Come again?" Sam's brows drew together.

"Memory ghosts…my father used to talk about them all the time. I think part of the reason he drank so much was to avoid them."

"Maybe I'm being completely obtuse, but I don't get it."

"Memory ghosts…you know, a certain song comes on the radio and it reminds you of your first kiss, or the scent of lilacs conjures a mental picture of your mother…every single time. You eat a banana split and you're right back in the ice cream parlor where Andy Stivick took you on your first real date….and you haven't given him a thought in years. Don't you see? That's what this is all about. That's what he was doing. He knew there would be some painful memories for me in this house, so he changed it completely. But the yard? It's almost an exact replica of when I was a child. He wanted me to remember the happy memories, the ones I wouldn't trade for anything. Before my mom died, before the drinking, before everything changed and went to hell. I mean there's no swing set, but I guess it would be a little silly at my age, huh? Anyway, when I saw it, something inside me snapped." She shrugged. "He always said the damn things sneak up on you when you least expect them."

She was no longer openly weeping, but tears continued to slip down her cheeks while she spoke so matter-of-factly about a heart shattered into a million pieces. At that moment, Madigan realized though it wouldn't always feel so sharp and fresh, she would live with the regret for the rest of her life. Her father tried so hard to make amends, but now he was truly gone and she'd missed her second chance. There would be no more memories to make. She'd nursed her resentment. She'd waited too long, wanting him to suffer as she had. It never occurred to her maybe he'd already done his share of suffering. It was a hard lesson to learn, but important lessons usually were, and there didn't seem to be any way around it, only right down the middle and through it.

Sam hunched forward and took her hand, regarding her intently. "I didn't know…about the yard, I mean.

I'd bet my life he didn't do it to make you feel bad. No matter what you might think of him, that wasn't Frank."

Maddie swiped at her wet cheeks with her free hand, then smiled, and gave his fingers a squeeze before pulling away.

"No, I don't think he did it to make me feel bad. Just the opposite. I think he wanted me to remember it had been different once. I've been feeling out of sorts since I arrived and maybe that's why. Somewhere deep down I did remember. As long as I didn't have to acknowledge it, I could hold on to my anger and ignore the grief. My therapist would probably tell me I needed to acknowledge my loss in order to move on." Maddie laughed mirthlessly. "I guess those sessions weren't a complete waste of time and money after all. The bottom line is I can't bring him back, and I suppose I'm only now realizing that. I'll always regret he never knew that somewhere deep down I did still love him. I'm not even sure I knew it myself until today."

"He knew," Sam said quietly.

"What makes you think so?"

"Do you think he would have gone to all this trouble, if he believed you'd written him off completely, and that you'd never come home?"

"I did consider it," she admitted honestly. "My initial instinct was to ignore it all, continue my life as though nothing had changed. Curiosity nibbled at me until I felt compelled to see how he'd lived, to find some hint of the man he'd become, or discover if there'd been anything left of the man I remembered." For so long she'd been yearning for a real home, a real family. Well, she'd waited too long and was left with only a house that used to be a home. Barely fifty percent of the equation.

"You're here now," Sam countered.

"Yeah, I guess. I don't think better late than never applies in this case. Why are you being so nice, anyway? We didn't exactly part on the best of terms."

"We didn't part on any terms at all, Maddie. One day you were just gone."

"Yeah, well, high school was over, and we weren't kids anymore. It was time to grow up. I got that scholarship to art school. You had a bright future ahead of you. We both know someone like me would only have held you back." Maddie shrugged and rose to her feet. "It all worked out for the best, right?"

"Someone like you?" He frowned. "I don't even understand what that's supposed to mean. Well, maybe someone like you didn't know as much about my future as you think."

"Or maybe someone like me understood the bigger picture a little better. It's ancient history, and we aren't those people anymore, right? Anyway, it sounds like you were a good friend to my father, which quite honestly boggles my mind a little, and you've been far nicer to me than I had any right to expect, so thanks."

"Well, if I heard you right, I think you mentioned something about food. Frozen entrees get pretty old. A good home-cooked meal would go a long way toward persuading me to forget all about that pesky little lamp to the skull incident. Make it dinner, and it's like it never happened."

"That sounds suspiciously like an offer I can't refuse," she smiled.

"You always were a smart girl." He climbed to his feet. "Tell you what. I'll run home, get cleaned up, and come back and get you. We'll grab a bite for lunch, then stop at the grocery store so you can get whatever you're gonna need for the next couple days, and then we'll decide what looks good for dinner. How does that sound?"

"Sounds great." Madigan glanced up and then choked back a laugh. It was no use. She erupted in a fit of giggles.

"What's so funny?" Sam demanded with narrowed eyes.

"Well." She coughed. "Not that you don't have the abs for it, but don't you think you're a little old for belly shirts?"

Sam glanced down and then his lips twisted in a self-conscious grin.

"Frank was a couple sizes smaller than me, I guess," he said by way of an explanation.

"And half a foot shorter," Maddie agreed. "The view is great, really…" Great enough, in fact, that her mouth felt peculiarly dry. In addition to the shirt riding up, his jeans had slipped down, resting low on his hips. Maddie's hungry eyes traced the tempting cord of muscle that made smart girls stupid sketching along his hips and disappearing into his waistband. She quickly looked away when she noticed the front of his jeans growing taut under her intense gaze. She was only here for a few weeks at best. It didn't seem wise even to contemplate adding another helping of complication to her already full plate.

"So, I'll see you in about an hour?" She wished she had something to occupy her hands. There weren't any odds and ends on the tables to straighten. Not even a magazine. Actually, though it was renovated beautifully, the entire place struck her as rather sterile. She finally settled for arranging the television remote neatly on the coffee table, then glanced at Sam.

"I guess Frank wasn't much for clutter. Not even a cheesy hunting scene over the fireplace. Oh well, I suppose the house will show better without a lot of personal bric-a-brac."

"Actually, we'd just finished painting this room a couple days before Frank...passed. Except for the furniture, everything is still piled upstairs. I guess you can go through it all and see if there's anything you want to keep. So you're really planning to sell?"

"Well, yeah, I guess so," Maddie replied slowly. "I mean, I already have a place, right? I have a job. I have friends. I have a life."

Maddie recognized she was trying to convince herself as much as she was trying to convince Sam. Sure, she had a place, but it was little more than somewhere to shower and sleep, and had never felt like a home. She had a job, two jobs in fact, both waiting tables to make ends meet. Not exactly a career. She had her painting, but she could do that anywhere. She had friends, friends who were so casual she honestly couldn't remember if she'd told anyone she would be away and she wasn't so sure anyone would notice she was gone. In fact, even her roommate, Chris, cared less about how long she'd be gone than about having the rent money paid in advance before Maddie left. A life she'd fallen into rather than one she'd consciously chosen.

"Right. Well, I know a real estate agent. I'll give him a call, and maybe he can stop by and check the place over if you want. I'll be back in about an hour, okay?" And with a quick wave, he was out the front door before she'd even had a chance to formulate a reply.

"Dammit, my life is somewhere else now, Sam," she whispered to the empty room, and wondered again who she was trying to convince.

"It doesn't have to be."

Maddie's heart lurched painfully, and her breath snagged in her throat. A chill started at the base of her spine and crawled the length of her back until the hair on her neck stood on end. The faint voice had come from behind her, over her left shoulder, and had been distinctly masculine. And disturbingly familiar. She spun, detecting the faint scent of cherry pipe tobacco, and faced an empty room. Her pulse beat a frantic tattoo. It was impossible! It was her overactive imagination's response to the emotional upheaval of the last few days and maybe a bit of wishful thinking. Or the remnants of sleep deprivation. Or maybe that can of soup last night had passed its expiration date. Spoiled food could make anyone hear voices, right?

Chapter Three

After Sam left, Madigan freshened up and then swallowed her trepidation and stepped out into the backyard again. Her throat still ached, but she'd regained her composure. Upon closer inspection, she realized the yard wasn't exactly the same. It was close enough that on first glance, it was like stepping from a time machine right into her childhood. She strolled out to the gazebo and cupped a lilac still heavy with unopened blossoms. Closing her eyes, she brought it to her face and inhaled deeply. The faint scent conjured visions of backyard barbecues and laughter and sweet, blissful innocence. She savored the small bubble of happiness the memories evoked. Maybe they would always be tinged with sadness, but if she was honest with herself—and all things considered, there didn't seem to be much sense in being anything else at this point—they hadn't been all bad. Somehow, even the ones that were didn't seem to hurt quite as much as they used to.

Her reverie came to an abrupt halt when she heard the sound of tires crunching in the drive. Sam was back and right on time. She shook off the shadows of her past and went through the house to the front door to let him in.

Maddie's stomach flipped when she opened the door to the fine figure of Sam Barstow propped against the doorjamb. In a clean pair of black jeans worn to exactly the right shade of faded, a snug black T-shirt, and a pair of lightly scuffed black boots, the guy was sex on a stick. Total Man Candy. An overt challenge to the will power of women everywhere. And Maddie had never been immune.

"You clean up well." She pushed open the storm door and waved him in. At least she'd taken the time to put on a little mascara, undo her ponytail, and brush out her hair. It tumbled over her shoulders in a loose, fragrant cloud. "Of course, now I feel like I'm underdressed."

Sam glanced down at himself and then back at her. "For the diner and grocery shopping? You look fine to me."

In fact, she looked better than fine, she looked positively edible. The way her top clung to her smallish but temptingly rounded breasts made him ache to reach out and cup one in his big hand just to test the fit. He had a hunch it would still be perfect. And when she turned her back on him and bent to retrieve her purse from the side of the couch, his jeans tightened, and his tongue stuck to the roof of his mouth at the sight of her heart-shaped ass molded lovingly by the denim. He couldn't shake the memory of what she'd felt like in his arms earlier. Every time he looked at her, desire struck him like a fist to the gut. The feeling was both unexpected and unwelcome.

He'd promised Frank he'd finish the house and help her out if she actually showed up. He hadn't been happy about it, especially after she'd rejected her father's overture. Frank waxed philosophical, but Sam sensed the man's quiet devastation. He decided, then and there, Madigan Moran was a self-centered, heartless bitch. Of course, he'd learned his lesson about her a long time ago. He hadn't expected, for one second, to be attracted to her still. Hell, he hadn't even expected to like her. And though he tried not to see it, she was struggling, too. Maybe she hadn't been indifferent to Frank after all, maybe she'd just been trying to protect a heart that had already been broken one too many times.

Shit! He needed to keep his distance. He didn't want these glimpses of the vulnerable, sweet girl who'd knocked him head over heels all those years ago. He had a feeling she could still get under his skin if he let her. Not a good idea. He didn't believe in happily-ever-after. Not anymore. He was, however, a firm believer in happily-for-now, and that could lead to complications neither of them needed. Her plan for selling the house and going back to her life was probably the best thing. For both of them. He didn't need another kick in the teeth any more than she needed another disappointment.

Sam heard the crunch of gravel in the drive and turned to see the long, sleek lines of Jeff Hagen's black convertible pulling in behind his car. Sam had called and asked him to stop over later in the day, or maybe tomorrow, but in the current real estate market, it was no surprise the agent wouldn't waste any time jumping on a potential listing.

"Hey, Jeff." Sam raised a hand in greeting while Madigan peeked over his shoulder to see who had arrived.

"The real estate agent I told you about," Sam explained. "I asked him to stop by later. I guess he didn't get to be the top salesman in three counties by sitting on his thumbs."

"Sam." The agent bounded onto the porch and briefly grasped the hand Sam offered. Then he turned and offered a hand to Maddie. "You must be Madigan. I'm Jeff Hagen. I understand you want to list this little gem."

"Uh, yeah," Maddie replied slowly. His hand held hers a little longer than Sam thought necessary. "Sam and I were on our way out. Maybe you could come back tomorrow?"

"Well, sure…I could, but this won't take long," he promised slickly. "I've already pulled the information on the place from the tax rolls, so I have all the details about the square footage and the lot size. Just need a ten cent tour to take a couple photos, get a feel for the place, and decide what selling points will get us the most bang for our buck."

Maddie glanced at Sam. He shrugged. He didn't know Jeff all that well. Their families had moved in the same social circles when they were kids, and now they played in the same softball league. The well-dressed agent exuded wealth and privilege. Sam could tell from Maddie's tense expression that he wasn't the only one whose teeth were on edge. Yeah, Jeff was a little pushy, a little self-absorbed, and a lot over the top, but you couldn't argue with a guy's sales record. If she really wanted to sell the place, all indications were Jeff Hagen was the man for the job.

"I'm in no hurry, Maddie. It's up to you." Sam said. "If you want to sell the place quickly, there isn't much point in waiting. Home sales suck at the moment. The sooner it's on the market, the better your chance of finding a buyer."

"My philosophy exactly!" Jeff concurred.

"Well, if you're sure it won't take long," Maddie allowed, stepping to one side to let Jeff enter.

"This place is great!" Jeff enthused as he took in the modern finishes in the kitchen and downstairs bath. He peered out the back door at the yard and made a few notes. He snapped a few pictures, then turned back toward the living room. "Three bedrooms, right?"

"Yeah, and two baths," Sam offered. Maddie followed slowly as Jeff sprinted up the stairs.

He glanced in the bathroom, nodded happily and scribbled in his notebook when Sam pointed out the laundry closet, then threw open the bedroom door nearest the bathroom.

Maddie hung back nervously. The room contained nothing but stacks of boxes. There were two large windows covered with curtains that, if she remembered correctly, would let in tons of great light. She couldn't help thinking the room would make a fantastic studio. It definitely had more potential than the cluttered corner of the small, dark, ten-by-ten bedroom in her apartment currently serving as both her living and workspace. Holding her breath, she reluctantly followed the men to the next room.

Her father's room was the same nondescript and typically masculine space it had always been. The furniture was old, the same suite her parents purchased when they first got married, and she remembered it well. There were boxes piled in this room, too, and Jeff made the observation that the house would show much better if the cartons were stashed out of sight. Maddie sighed. She knew she'd have to go through them eventually, but didn't relish the prospect. Maybe she could move everything into the attic for the time being? She followed the men back out of the room. The tour concluded in the front bedroom. Hers. Her emotions had been up and down like a roller coaster all day, and if her reaction to the back yard was any indication, she was pretty sure she wasn't ready to see it again for the first time in years with witnesses present. She hung back in the hallway, ignoring Sam's questioning gaze. The click of a door suggested the agent was checking out the closet space. He emerged back into the hallway and jotted down a few more notes before they all headed back downstairs.

"Great view of the yard from that window," he observed. "Too bad there isn't an attached bath to make it a true master, but that's not uncommon in these older homes. Unfinished concrete basement, right?" Maddie turned to Sam, who nodded and took the lead as they headed back down to the kitchen and continued into the basement.

Jeff Hagen immediately noticed the narrow basement windows were propped open a crack and a dehumidifier hummed in the corner.

"The basement floods?" He cocked a knowing brow in Sam's direction.

"Not unless we get several days of heavy rain, but it does stay pretty damp down here," Sam confirmed.

"Well, with the high water table in this area, it's a common enough problem but certainly not a deal breaker. Just better to have all the facts in the interest of full disclosure. Don't want the buyer coming back at us later claiming we tried to misrepresent anything." Jeff took a few measurements, checked the condition of the furnace and the metal doors covering the concrete steps of the walk-out leading to the back yard, and then waved them toward the stairs to indicate he was finished.

"Okay, that should do it." Jeff smiled after confirming there was also an unfinished walkup attic and writing down Maddie's name and phone number. He pulled a sheaf of papers from his clipboard and scribbled down a figure. He held it under Maddie's nose, and Sam leaned over her shoulder to take a look. "Based on comparables, I think this is a fair asking price. I can tell you while this is a great place, it's probably been over-improved for the neighborhood, and you won't get as much for it as you would if it was out by the lake. I still think we should be able to get top dollar. Just leave everything to me."

"Um, okay?" Hagen's slick salesmanship rubbed her the wrong way, but Sam seemed to think he was the man for the job, and what did she know about real estate?

Sam shrugged noncommittally. "Seems like a fair price."

"Okay, then! If we're all in agreement, I took the liberty of preparing the contracts in advance." He tugged yet more papers from the pile. "All I need to do is plug in the price and you can sign on the dotted line. Why don't you read through them while I grab a sign and a lock-box from the car?"

He placed the paperwork on the kitchen table and headed for the front door. Maddie collapsed on a chair and pulled the contracts toward her. She looked at Sam uncertainly. It was all happening so fast. But wasn't that exactly what she'd wanted when she arrived?

"He doesn't waste any time, does he? What do you

think?"

"If you want to sell, I think Jeff's the guy who can get it done. Your house, your call."

Maddie stared at the paperwork and drummed her fingers on the table. Finally, she grabbed the pen and scribbled her signature on the contract before she had a chance to change her mind. Sam simply turned and walked over to stare out the back door without comment.

She heard Jeff on the front porch and gathered the papers into a neat pile. She carried them into the parlor, and after a slight hesitation, Sam followed. Jeff held a small box in his hands and, through the open front door, Maddie could see he'd also taken the liberty of planting a For Sale sign in the front yard. Yep, he definitely rubbed her the wrong way, but at least he seemed like a go-getter.

She handed the papers to Jeff, who glanced down and then favored her with a smile.

"Excellent! Sam wasn't sure how long you planned to stay, but that's not a problem. If we find a buyer in the meantime, we'll negotiate a closing date that suits you. Now all I need is an extra house key for the lock-box so when we put the house on the multi-list service the other agents have access to show the place."

Maddie turned to Sam again. Before she could ask, he fished a key ring from his pocket and worked one free, tossing it to Jeff.

"I didn't mean for you to give him your key," Maddie protested.

Sam lifted a shoulder. "I still have mine. Not that I'll need it, now you're home. That's your dad's. Yours is an extra the lawyer had made."

"Oh."

Jeff Hagen punched a code into a small electronic device to open the box and drop the key inside. He bent and secured it to the knob of the front door, and turned back with a grin.

"Okay, all set."

"Thanks for coming out, Jeff." Sam moved toward the front door and stuck out a hand. It was a clear dismissal. "Will you be at the game next week?"

"Hey, no problem, man." Jeff took the hand and hesitated near the door. "Not sure. I have an open house over in Greeley. Depends on what time I get everything wrapped up. May have to quit the league altogether. Seems like it gets harder and harder to make the games. People work all week, they want their agent available on the weekends."

"Yeah, I guess they would. Well, thanks again." Sam put a hand on the man's shoulder, and Maddie could have sworn he gave Jeff a slight shove toward the door.

"Nice meeting you, Madigan." Jeff waved cheerily as he stumbled over the doorjamb onto the porch. "I'll be in touch."

"Thank you," Maddie responded politely. Sam waited until Jeff slid behind the wheel of the low-slung speed machine and revved the engine, then turned back to Maddie with a faint frown.

"Ready?"

"Just let me grab my phone." Maddie went into the kitchen and grabbed the phone from the counter where she'd left it to charge. Glancing down at the display, she frowned. Three missed calls, all from the same number. Ian Sutherland's number. She deleted them and shoved the phone in her pocket. Then she hurried back to the living room, and Sam.

He held the door and waited while she locked it. Her eyes widened as she spotted the car, and when she reached it, he held the door for her again. She climbed in with a grin.

"He's a little, um, enthusiastic, huh?"

"He's downright overbearing," Sam agreed. "But he has the best sales record of anyone I know. Nothing but the best for you, kid."

"I see that." She patted the dashboard of the vintage black Mustang and smiled at him as he folded his long length into the driver's seat. "I can't believe you still have her, although I must say, she looks a hell of a lot better in paint than she ever did in that awful gray primer."

"Yeah, well…I usually drive the truck, but I figured you might like to get out of the vehicle as clean as you were when you got in it."

"Well, since I brought a very limited wardrobe, I appreciate it." She cleared her throat. "So what are you doing with yourself these days?"

"Puttering," he replied. He glanced over and waggled his brows like a movie villain. "I always was good with my hands."

"Another of your impossible to resist pick-up lines?" She laughed.

"Well, that depends. Is it working?"

"Not yet," she retorted. "But don't let it keep you from trying. So, where do you find the time? I mean, being a corporate big wig must be pretty time consuming all by itself."

"I imagine it would be." Sam shrugged and seemed

suddenly very interested in the road.

"Would be? You didn't like being a vice president?"

"What?"

"Barstow Enterprises…You didn't like working for your father?"

"Hell, Maddie, I never intended to work for my father. You knew that." His brows drew together in a dark frown.

"But your father…" His father had insisted that going into the family business was exactly what Sam would do. He also made it crystal clear she was nothing more than a lapse in judgment. His son would never throw away his future for a teenage infatuation with the daughter of a blue collar drunk, no matter what Sam might have told her.

"My father is an arrogant bully who couldn't conceive his son wouldn't do exactly what he wanted him to do," Sam replied in a clipped tone. "He still can't."

"So then what did you do…after I left?" Her voice came out in a strangled whisper, and she coughed hard to clear the uncomfortable tightness from her throat.

"Did a stint in the service, then went to school for law enforcement, exactly as I'd planned. Worked a couple years in executive protection," he responded in a curt tone that didn't exactly invite further discussion.

"Executive protection?" She wasn't sure if it was nerves or the fact it just hit home that Sam apparently hadn't lied to her, but his father sure as hell had. Whatever the reason, his career choice struck her as incredibly funny. "I'm sorry, that sounds like a particularly exclusive brand of condoms."

Sam glanced over at her and then back at the road. The corners of his lips twitched.

"Not exactly," he said at last.

"Okay, so what is it…exactly?"

"Personal security. Witness protection. That kind of thing."

"Oh, you mean like a bodyguard or something?"

"Yeah, like a bodyguard or something."

"So, you're between jobs at the moment, or what?" She was astute enough to sense his reluctance to elaborate, but suddenly she needed to know. All these years she'd been convinced she'd made the right decision for everyone when she walked away. Though, the more he talked, the clearer it became there was every possibility she'd let Edward Barstow induce her to do exactly the wrong thing, while persuading her she was doing it for all the right reasons.

"I guess that's one way of looking at it." Sam slowed the car and his eyes narrowed as he scanned the street. "Retired, actually."

"Aren't you a little young to be collecting Social Security?"

"Some things age you a hell of a lot faster than others," he replied quietly.

****

Sam expertly maneuvered into a parking space in front of Caroline's. He turned off the ignition, heaved a deep sigh, and turned to face her. Now she would ask what happened. People always did. And if she asked, he decided he would tell her because she'd had little enough reason to trust people in her life and he found that for a man who'd been prepared to dislike her on sight, he wanted her to trust him. Pointless, since once she learned the whole truth, she would probably run from him as far and as fast as she could. Her opinion hadn't mattered to him much when he still believed she was nothing but a shallow bitch, yet he couldn't shake the uncomfortable feeling maybe he'd had her all wrong, maybe he'd missed something. Sam's jaw was clenched so tightly it ached, and he made a conscious effort to relax when he realized his shoulders were hunched nearly to his ears.

"Bummer," she said simply.

"What?" He blinked, nonplussed.

"I said that's a bummer." She shrugged. "You ended up doing what you wanted to do, and then it didn't turn out the way you hoped."

"You aren't even curious?" He couldn't believe she was letting him off the hook so easily. He also couldn't believe he was looking a gift horse in the mouth and belaboring the point. If he had half a brain, he'd shut the hell up and let it go.

"Well, sure I'm curious." She shrugged again. "C'mon, who understands better than me there are some things that aren't so easy to talk about? Do you think I just open my mouth and tell everyone I meet about *my* life? If you want to tell me, tell me. If you don't, that's your prerogative. It's not as if you owe me an explanation. In fact, it's not as if you owe me anything. But do you think can you decide over lunch? I'm starving."

She raised her brows, then waggled them just as he had.

Every good intention of keeping his distance suddenly evaporated. Unable to resist, Sam impulsively leaned over and cupped his fingers around her nape, pulling her across the seat and settling his mouth on hers. She initially stiffened in surprise, then relaxed and opened her lips willingly when his tongue tentatively traced the seam of hers seeking entry. He knew he'd regret it later. She would probably read something into it. He ignored the little voice in his head asking him what the hell he was doing and concentrated instead on the feel of her soft, pliable lips under his, the faint lemony scent of her hair, and the soft brush of her fingertips as she reached a hand to trace it along his jaw. Damn, she tasted even better than he remembered. She scooted closer, leaning over the console, and he deepened the kiss, slanting his mouth over hers, repeatedly, until both of them were breathing raggedly, and he knew it would be at least a few minutes before he could comfortably and modestly climb from the car. He pulled back reluctantly when it finally dawned on him that they were parked in front of the busiest diner in town at lunchtime, necking like the two horny teenagers they used to be. Talk about a memory ghost. What in the hell was he thinking? He hadn't intended for a simple kiss to go so far. In fact, he hadn't even intended a simple kiss. Damn.

"Maybe I've been going about things all wrong." Maddie slowly sat back against her own seat, watching him with a bemused expression that didn't completely obliterate the hint of wariness in her eyes.

"What?"

"Well, usually when I meet an attractive man, I dazzle him with my wit and baffle him with my brilliance." She chuckled. "Yeah, that doesn't usually work out so well. Who knew the secret all along was to conk him over the head with a lamp and threaten him with a hammer?"

Sam blinked, then threw back his head in a long, full-throated laugh. He'd happily take a baseball bat to his head to kiss her like that again and see that slumberous promise in her eyes. Shit, he was in so much trouble.

"C'mon, woman, I promised you lunch."

"I hope you know what you've gotten yourself into, mister. I haven't had anything except soup and crackers since yesterday morning," she retorted, yanking the door handle and climbing out before he could come around to open the door. "And I always did have a healthy appetite."

Chapter Four

Maddie snorted when her feet struck the pavement and she had to grab onto the door for support. Good Lord, the man could still kiss. If he could make her weak at the knees with a kiss, what could he do if he got a few other body parts involved? She shouldn't even be thinking about it. She wouldn't be here very long, and it would just further complicate things. Then again, they both knew she would be leaving so there was no chance of anything but a casual fling, right? Of course, she and Sam had never been casual, at least on her part, no matter what she'd tried to sell herself on the bus out of town. She'd been on the Bad Boyfriend Tour ever since. At least she knew Sam Barstow might be worth the high price of a ticket.

"Did you just snort?" he called across the hood, narrowing his eyes.

"Don't be silly, Sam. A lady never snorts." She circled the car and linked her arm through his as though it was the most natural thing in the world. He stiffened but didn't pull away.

"Hmm, well I think I recognize a snort when I hear one. I bet you snore, too."

"Wouldn't you like to know?" she retorted.

"I think I'll plead the fifth." He frowned and tugged her toward the door.

The diner was crowded when they entered. Maddie

hadn't come here often, but it hadn't changed much from what she remembered. In fact, she suspected it hadn't changed much since it opened fifty years ago. A long bar with red vinyl stools ran the length of one wall, facing the tall, wooden booths lining the opposite side of the long, narrow room. Lighted cases of chrome and glass held an assortment of decadent desserts. Down the center of the floor stood a double row of square tables covered with red-checkered tablecloths and crammed with people. The ceiling was made of painted tin panels and dotted with wobbly, overworked ceiling fans turning in crooked circles. The wood plank floors were scuffed and worn and had seen better days. Actually, the entire place looked as though it had seen better days, but everything was scrupulously clean and Maddie figured the crush of people and the mouthwatering aromas were a testament to the food quality.

As they stood in the doorway, people waved to Sam and called out over the din of conversation and clinking cutlery. He nodded back with a smile, but stayed glued to Maddie's side. Several people craned their necks to stare at Maddie with an undisguised curiosity that made her palms sweat and her stomach churn, but she didn't see anyone she recognized. A group stood to exit a booth near the back, and Sam quickly steered Maddie toward it with a hand on her back. She slid into the red vinyl bench seat on the side facing away from the rest of the diners, and Sam slid into the other. A middle-aged waitress with an outrageous shade of yellow hair, bundled haphazardly into a hair net, hurriedly waddled toward them with a gray plastic bin tucked under one arm. Her uniform matched her hair, and her eyes were heavily shadowed in a shocking blue. Her bright red lipstick extended at least a quarter inch beyond her lip line giving her a garish, clown-like appearance. She chomped a wad of gum to the beat of her footsteps, and her bulbous plastic earrings bobbed along with the rhythm of her jaw.

"Morning, Sam." She smiled, plunking the plastic bin on the table and quickly and efficiently filling it with the stacks of dirty dishes from the booth's previous occupants. "I'll have this cleared off in a sec." She leaned across the table and pulled two laminated menus from behind a chrome napkin dispenser, handing one first to Maddie and then to Sam.

"'Morning, Caroline." Sam smiled back. "Don't know if you remember Madigan Moran, Frank's daughter?"

"The famous artist?" Caroline fixed a stare on Maddie with unabashed interest. "Haven't seen you since you were a little girl."

"More of a struggling artist, I'm afraid." Maddie offered her a shy smile, having no recollection of the woman at all.

"Not according to Frank. Sorry about your dad, honey. We sure do miss him. Turkey club and root beer float twice a week. Meat loaf every Sunday. Such a shame you were out of the country and had to miss the funeral, but I'm sure he'd understand. What with your career and all."

"What—" Sam kicked Maddie's shin lightly under the table. Out of the country? The closest she'd ever come to being out of the country was a vacation at Point Pleasant Beach when she swam out past the buoy and had to be rescued by the lifeguard from a rip current trying to carry her out to sea. Where had the woman gotten the idea she wasn't at the funeral because she was out of the country? And what did she mean *not according to Frank*? Had her father actually bragged to people about her? Great. Now she had a reputation to live up to. Well, she wouldn't be here long enough for it to matter. Caroline, the waitress, continued to regard her expectantly.

"Oh, err, thank you. I'm sorry I wasn't able to be here," Maddie replied quietly.

"Frank was a helluva guy, he would have understood, like I said. Well, I'll give you a couple minutes to check out the menu," Caroline offered, cracking her gum. "Sam, you having your usual?"

"Sounds good." Sam snapped his menu closed and tucked it back behind the napkins.

"What's your usual?" Maddie asked curiously, scanning the menu quickly.

"Grilled cheese with bacon and tomato on french toast, fries with beef gravy on the side, and a chocolate milkshake." He grinned like a little boy who'd been handed a bag of candy.

"Do you ever actually *hear* your arteries screaming while you eat?" Maddie raised a brow. She snapped the menu closed and tucked it in with Sam's. "I'll have the same."

"Easy-peasy." Caroline jotted the order on her notepad, heaved the bin off the table with one beefy arm, and reached into the pocket of her apron to swipe a damp rag over the tabletop with the other. "I'll be back with your drinks. Nice to meet you, Madigan."

"Nice to meet you too," Maddie responded politely. As soon as the woman was out of earshot, she leaned across the table and whispered to Sam. "Out of the country? Where would anyone get the idea I wasn't at the funeral because I was out of the country?"

Sam fixed his gaze somewhere over her head and tugged at the neck of his shirt as a dark flush crept up his neck and into his face. Maddie continued to stare at him with her brows raised.

"Well," he began uncomfortably, "I might have told people something to that effect."

"What in the hell for?" Maddie demanded hotly.

"People in this town liked your father, Madigan," Sam explained in a low tone. "They felt bad when he died. They wouldn't understand a daughter who didn't show for her father's funeral. Frank wouldn't have wanted you to be judged by people before they got a chance to know you."

"Well, anyone who still remembers me or what my life was like when my father was drinking sure as hell shouldn't judge me. Why? Why would you care what people thought of me, Sam? It seems to me like you have less reason than anyone to give a flying fig about my reputation," Maddie asked suspiciously. People weren't nice without an ulterior motive in her experience. Nonetheless, she wanted Sam to be someone she could still take at face value. It made no sense, but there it was.

"Even at his worst, your father was a functional alcoholic, Maddie. He paid his bills, held down a job, never caused a scene in public. Sure, maybe a few people knew he liked to have one too many, but most people had no idea what your day-to-day life was really like. Anyway, I didn't do it for you, I did it for your father. He wanted you to have a life here if you wanted one. How well do you think that would have worked out if people had a reason to dislike you before you ever arrived?"

"What about you? What did you think of a daughter who didn't show for her father's funeral?"

"I knew the truth," he said quietly. "I understood what you'd been through with him, maybe better than most."

"You think I'm a terrible person," Maddie announced with certainty.

"No, I don't think you're a terrible person. I think you're a person who did what she felt she needed to do," Sam sighed. "That's all anybody can do, I guess."

"Well, thank you. I know you didn't do it for me, but it was good of you to worry about my father."

"I told you, I liked your father. I owed him. The least I could do was give you a chance to make your own impression for his sake."

"Well, it might make a difference if I was staying, but I'm not."

"You can hardly call twenty-four hours giving the place a chance."

"A chance for what? He wanted me to have security? Okay, I get it now, and I appreciate it. If I sell the house and bank the money, I have that same security, right? I don't need much. Besides, what would I do here?" Maddie sighed and looked around. Pine Grove hadn't changed much from the town she remembered, and something about it tugged at her heart despite her automatic protestations.

"The same things you do now. Work, paint," Sam returned reasonably. "Attack attractive men with improvised weapons."

Maddie smiled automatically and shook her head without looking at him. She couldn't abandon her life and move to Pine Grove because…well, she couldn't, that's all. She turned back to Sam and cleared her throat.

"How did he die, Sam?" She'd been telling herself it didn't matter from the moment she heard the news, but she suddenly had to ask, even though she feared the answer. Sam sighed and sat back against the booth staring down at the tabletop.

"I went over to work on the house and found him in his bed. I like to think it was peaceful. He looked like he'd fallen asleep, and just never woke up. We both knew it was only a matter of time. Even though he'd stopped drinking, he'd already done the damage to his liver. When the liver isn't working, the blood finds another route, usually through veins that can't take the pressure. Sometimes they rupture and bleed."

"Didn't they know that could happen?"

Sam nodded.

"Yes. He had a small bleeding episode about two years ago. The doctor recommended a shunt procedure to insert a tube and reduce the pressure."

"It didn't work?"

"He refused to have it done."

"Maybe if I'd come sooner…" Maddie began in a strangled voice. "Maybe…" Maybe if she'd been willing to give him another chance, he would have tried harder to save his own life. Maybe she could have given him a reason to fight. Maybe…

"Look, Maddie, any regrets you have about your relationship with Frank…that's something you have to come to terms with on your own. But this? Not something you need to lose sleep over. You coming back might have given him a little more peace of mind at the end, but I doubt it would have changed the outcome. The shunt reduces the pressure, but it leads to a shitload of other complications. It's not a cure, it's a last ditch effort. Frank fought hard to get his life back and decided he'd rather have his wits about him for whatever time he had left. If you remember anything about the man he was before the booze, you know he would have made the same decision whether you were here or not."

Maddie traced a pattern on the table with her fingertip and nodded slowly. The man her father had been would have made the same choice. But it was painful to remember that man because it forced her to face the loss. It was easier to remember the man she'd grown to resent, but the more she learned, the harder it became.

"You keep saying you owed my father. Owed him for what? Why did he specify in his will that I had to at least visit the place again before selling?" She looked up and met Sam's gaze, surprising a flash of sympathy in those deep, blue eyes.

"He helped me through a bad patch once." Sam leaned back in the booth as Caroline approached. "And he wanted you to visit before selling because he hoped you'd come to love it here again as much as he did and decide to stay."

Any further interrogation was temporarily halted by the arrival of their milkshakes. Caroline placed a tall, aluminum shaker in front of each of them. A thin coating of ice clung to the sides and small rivulets of condensation streaked their way to the tabletop to form a ring of moisture at the base. The shake was so thick that the straw stood on its own when Maddie unwrapped it and poked it in. It took a bit of effort to suck the thick, frosty concoction into her mouth, but when she got her first good taste, she closed her eyes and let out a moan of sheer delight. Sam didn't bother with a straw and simply grabbed the large, frosty container, brought it to his lips, and took a huge gulp Maddie knew would have given her instant brain freeze. He seemed completely unaffected as he observed her obvious pleasure. Clearly, he was not a milkshake virgin.

"Oh my God," she moaned again. "How did I live here all those years and never have one of these? What do they put in these things? This is fantastic!"

"Didn't have them back then. Caroline worked here as a waitress, and then she bought the place when old man Herron died. She changed the entire menu. The milkshake is her own concoction. Uses dark chocolate gelato instead of ice cream and half-heavy cream instead of milk. Rumor has it there's some other deep, dark, family-secret ingredient, but no one's ever figured out what it is," he whispered before swallowing another large mouthful.

"I think maybe I could live on these," she sighed, dipping in a spoon to help her along.

"What were you saying earlier about screaming arteries?" Sam asked with a teasing glint in his eyes.

"I didn't say I *would*, I said I *could*."

"Not to mention what a steady diet of those would do to your rather remarkable figure."

"So you've graduated from bad pick-up lines to backhanded compliments?"

"Is it an improvement?"

"Haven't decided." Maddie smirked and let her gaze wander, wondering what was taking their order so long to arrive. She'd been hungry to begin with and the pervasive smell of food only aggravated her grumbling tummy. The crowd wasn't thinning at all. In fact, a small knot of people had congregated by the door waiting for tables and occasionally glanced impatiently at their watches. Caroline dashed between the tables like a madwoman; taking orders, slinging plates, and trying to bus and clean the tables all at once. Damp wisps of canary yellow hair had escaped from her hairnet and clung moistly to her neck and forehead. Her jaws worked her gum a mile a minute and her smile appeared forced as she tried to do it all and keep everyone happy. Her eyes broadcast her desperation. Maddie knew that look. She'd worked short on more than one occasion herself.

"Doesn't she have any help?" Maddie wrinkled her forehead in concern. Orders piled up in the window between the kitchen and the dining room. At least four cluttered tables needed clearing. Three people tried to flag the harried woman down for drink refills and a couple of others were demanding their checks.

Sam craned his neck and swiveled his head from side to side. "Doesn't appear so. Someone must have called in sick. There's never only one waitress at lunchtime."

Maddie's fingers drummed restlessly on the tabletop as she watched Caroline. Spooning a large portion of milkshake into her mouth to hold her over, she slid out of the booth.

"Be right back," she promised.

"Hey, where are you going?"

Maddie walked to the end of the bar and checked behind it. The gray bins were exactly where she'd expected them to be. There was a sink next to the stack of bins and she grabbed a dishcloth, rinsed it under the water, and squeezed out the excess. She grabbed a bin and headed for a table. She made short work of clearing the dishes and wiping the surface before moving on to the next. When the bin was filled, she pushed the swinging door to the kitchen open with her backside and set the dirty dishes on the first counter she saw. Then she grabbed another bin and repeated the process. Once she cleared all the cluttered tables, she started on the drink refills. To her relief, she noticed the tables had small enameled numbers on the base. Should make it easy to match with the orders. She moved to the kitchen window and grabbed a check from the metal carousel. She checked the items, matched them to the plates waiting under the heat lamps, and loaded them onto a tray. Then she started delivering food to the hungry customers. She grabbed her order and Sam's then deposited them on their table. She paused to take another gulp of her milkshake and gobble down a couple fries dipped in gravy.

"What in the hell do you think you're doing?" Sam asked in a deceptively mild tone that did little to hide his amusement.

Maddie dragged her forearm across her moist brow wishing she'd left her hair tied back. "Helping? Don't wait for me. Go ahead and eat. I'll be right back."

Caroline noticed the cleared tables and stopped in her tracks when she saw Maddie in action. She caught her eye and offered her a grateful smile. Maddie smiled back. Within ten minutes, order had been restored, everyone was taken care of, and the weary waitress with the Big Bird hair had things well in control. Maddie lifted her hair off the back of her neck to cool herself and slid back into the booth opposite Sam.

She noticed that with the exception of a couple fries, his food remained untouched. He'd waited for her, anyway.

"I told you to go ahead and eat," she protested. "Now your food is cold."

"So is yours," he observed pointedly.

"I'm so hungry at this point I doubt I'll taste it anyway. There must be a microwave in the kitchen. Let me see if they'll reheat it for you." She reached for his plate and he slid it to the side.

"Sit down and eat, Madigan. I'm good."

****

Cold food wasn't a concern for Sam, but the overwhelming attraction he was feeling toward Madigan Moran sure as hell was. He wanted to cling to his expectations and preconceived notions of what the woman who walked out on him would be like, but she contradicted them at every turn. In his mind, he had her all figured out, but his heart and his gut were ignoring his head. And he knew better than to listen to either of those things. They'd steered him wrong before and cost him nearly everything. He wasn't about to make the same mistake again.

Chapter Five

Maddie and Sam consumed their lukewarm food, making polite small talk in between bites about people she'd known or gone to high school with. Maddie learned the few friends she'd briefly considered touching base with had brushed off the dust of small town life and moved away long ago. She swallowed the fleeting sense of disappointment along with the last mouthful of her milkshake. After all, she'd left too, right?

Sam had no sooner mopped up the remaining gravy and popped the last fry into his mouth when Caroline approached the table with two enormous pieces of white layer cake covered in buttercream and coconut, and two fragrant, steaming mugs of coffee.

"Caroline, you are a goddess," Sam exhaled on an appreciative sigh.

"Common knowledge, honey," she concurred with a chuckle. She turned to Maddie with a grateful smile. "But this girl? She is an angel. Thanks for your help, doll. I was about ready to blow an aneurysm."

"Been there, done that." Maddie laughed. "I recognized the look."

"Well, I can't tell you how much I appreciate it. On the house." She set the cake on the table with a flourish.

"Oh, but…" Maddie began.

"That's not necessary, Caroline," Sam protested.

"Hey, Pretty Boy, my restaurant, my rules." Caroline's penciled brows drew together. "Gloria not only called off this morning, she called back later to say she quit. Kids! No work ethic or sense of responsibility anymore. This week is going to be hell. Brenda is picking up some extra shifts, but it's hard for her with the baby and all."

As Caroline talked, Maddie's fingers began drumming insistently on the table again, and Sam glanced over wondering what was brewing in that beautiful head of hers. He'd damn near swallowed his teeth when she suddenly hopped up and simply went to work. She'd seemed so timid and self-conscious when they first walked in, but when Caroline was drowning, Maddie was the only one who dove in to offer her a life preserver without a second thought.

"Caroline," Maddie drawled in a thoughtful tone. "I'm going to be here for the next few weeks anyway, and I don't have all that much to do at the house to get it ready for sale. I'm not used to sitting around and twiddling my thumbs, and I don't think I'll be very good at it."

"How do you know what you have to do to get the house ready for sale? You haven't even started yet. Hell, you've barely worked up the courage to go upstairs," Sam mumbled with an audible snort.

"Did you say something, Sam?" Maddie shot a dark look in his direction before turning her attention back to Caroline. "So, I was thinking, maybe I can come over and give you a hand for an hour or two at lunchtime a couple days a week, at least 'til you find someone or it's time for me to leave. I have quite a bit of experience. What do you think?"

Caroline looked stunned. And that was nothing compared to the expression Sam knew he sported. He sure hoped he'd be able to pick his jaw up from the floor, otherwise he was going to have a real problem eating his cake.

"Well, I…I don't know what to say, Madigan," Caroline sputtered.

"Once you get to know her better you'll realize how rare that is." Sam grinned.

Caroline reached out and swatted his shoulder.

Well, I guess it's true I'm rarely at a loss for words," she conceded with a laugh. "We only do breakfast and lunch, and breakfast isn't so bad. But lunch, well…I'd be awfully grateful for the help. I can't pay you much. What about your painting and all?"

"Tell you what, minimum wage, tips, and lunch on the days I work, and we'll call it even. As for my painting…technically, I'm on vacation and didn't even bring any supplies."

She did, however, have a crate of her paintings in transit that should be arriving any day. She'd had the pieces shipped here because there wasn't an inch of space left to store them in her apartment, and she didn't know what else to do when she impulsively yanked them from Ian's gallery. She would have paid a small fortune to see Ian's reaction when he realized the pieces were gone and she'd discovered the truth. Then she decided she didn't much care. There were always other galleries, and though she hadn't honestly intended to do any painting while she was here, the town did have its charm. And that rear bedroom had studio written all over it.

Maddie leaned closer and lowered her voice.

"Caroline, between you and me, it's possible my father may have exaggerated my fame just a tad. I sell something now and then. The Pope hasn't called to ask me to paint any chapel ceilings or anything like that."

"Well, it sounds like a win-win situation for me. But, honey, you shouldn't underestimate yourself. Your work is wonderful!" Caroline enthused.

"You've seen my work?" Maddie gaped.

"Well, yeah! That painting of your father's. I don't think I've ever seen a man prouder of anything in my life." She smiled brightly and nodded. "Isn't that right, Sam?"

"Oh, uh, right!" Sam grabbed his fork and dug into the cake as though he hadn't eaten in a week. He didn't raise his eyes the entire time Caroline and Maddie worked out a schedule. He smiled and kept eating when Caroline refused to bring them a bill for their meal. And then he became inordinately interested in his coffee when Caroline finally moved away to another table.

"The painting's upstairs, isn't it?" Maddie expelled a resigned sigh.

Sam set the cup down and sighed too. "Yup."

"You know, Sam, you could warn me about these things so I don't get blindsided," she muttered. "Out of the country, famous artist, painting over the fireplace...anything else about my so-called life I should be aware of? Is Elvis living in my closet? Do I know where Jimmy Hoffa is buried?" She stabbed the cake with her fork and hefted a bite into her mouth in exasperation, moaning and rolling her eyes in delight as she registered the taste filling her mouth.

"How was I supposed to know you were going to volunteer for waitress duty and get all chummy with

Caroline when I brought you out for lunch?"

"Hey, I'm simply charming like that. By the way, is there somewhere I can get a bus schedule? Of course, I can probably just as easily walk as long as the weather is decent."

"No problem. I usually eat here when I'm in town anyway. I can run you back and forth until the car is ready." Maddie was uncomfortably aware that Sam stared as though fascinated with her mouth as she chewed and swallowed another bite of cake. A stray strand of coconut stuck to the corner of her lip, and her tongue snaked out to capture it. He coughed forcefully and looked away.

"You're sure?"

"Told you this morning, I mean what I say."

"Well, okay then, if you're sure."

"Did I say I was sure?"

"Well, yeah, but…wait a minute. What car?"

"Frank's. Actually, I guess it's yours. Dropped it at the garage for a tune-up and inspection. Told them there was no hurry since you wouldn't be here until next week."

"I have a car?" Maddie grinned slowly. It had never been an issue in the city where public transportation was the norm. But to have one while she was here gave her a whole, new level of independence.

"Yep. Don't get too excited. It's not new or anything, but he always kept it well maintained, and it'll get you from point A to point B without a problem." Sam popped a last bite of cake into his mouth and laid his fork across the empty plate.

"Okay." She pushed back the cake remaining on her plate with a groan. "Not that I have any desire whatsoever to even think of food at the moment, but I guess it's time to hit the grocery store?"

"Well, you *did* promise me dinner as a condition of my not pressing assault charges."

"I don't remember the conversation *quite* that way, but I guess a deal is a deal." Maddie laughed. "I never eat this much for lunch. Actually, I usually skip it altogether. I think maybe I should have packed my fat pants."

"Your *what*?" Sam burst out laughing.

"My fat pants. Surely, you've heard of them. Every woman owns at least one pair," she said very seriously.

"If you say so." He chuckled as his eyes did a once-over. "But I can't see why you'd need them."

"If I keep eating like this every day while I'm here, I'll need a muumuu by Saturday." Maddie looked down at herself worriedly as though thunder thighs and a potbelly might suddenly appear. She slid out of the booth, and Sam tossed a couple bills on the table even though Caroline had insisted everything was on the house. Sam kept his hand on the small of Maddie's back as they wove between the tables. She felt his heat like a brand through the thin cotton of her top. She knew the gesture was probably nothing more than good, old-fashioned courtesy, but his light touch induced reactions her body had no business feeling. He guided her toward his car, only removing his hand from her back when he opened the door and ushered her in. While he jogged over to the driver's side, Maddie fought to rein in her galloping heart.

"You still like Italian food?" she asked breathlessly as he climbed behind the wheel. "I could do lasagna."

At the moment, she couldn't imagine even being

able to eat a bite, but it was something she made often and well. It was an easy dish to portion out and freeze, perfect to reheat for a quick dinner after a long day on her feet at work.

"That would be great if it isn't a lot of trouble. We could easily toss a couple of steaks on the grill and throw a salad together." He offered, swinging back out into the Main Street traffic.

"I don't do grills, so then you'd be making dinner, and that wasn't the deal. Besides, lasagna is one of my best dishes. Maybe I'm trying to impress you." She gave him a shy, sidelong glance and was gratified to see the dimple flash.

"You did that a long time ago."

Despite the quick smile, he didn't sound particularly happy about it. Unsure quite what to say, Maddie retreated into silence for the rest of the short drive to the market. Her eyes missed nothing as they passed through the center of town. She'd always admired the late Victorian architecture, beautiful detailing, and overall appeal of the well-tended buildings crowded together around a central square, and was happy to see it hadn't changed much. The storefronts were a charming mix of cafes, antique shops, and funky boutiques and she promised herself she would check them out the first chance she got. She also made a mental note to check into the small, unobtrusive gallery she noticed on the corner, too. It couldn't hurt to explore new markets, right? She didn't have her portfolio with her, but she did have scans of all her paintings on her laptop.

The square itself boasted a simple, yet elegant fountain surrounded by benches where mothers sat and gossiped together while laughing children splashed in the sun-sparkled spray. The scene tugged at her and her fingers itched to sketch it. The town was small, and Maddie knew she could probably walk to the square from the house in less than fifteen minutes until the car was ready. She wasn't especially comfortable relying on Sam for transportation. She wasn't accustomed to depending on anyone but herself.

The market was far less crowded than the diner had been. It wasn't large, but it was neat, well stocked, and brightly lit. It had gotten warm outside, and Maddie lingered in the frozen foods section enjoying the coolness even though she didn't buy many frozen items. She preferred fresh when she could get it. Sadly, it was too late in the day to make her own meat sauce, which she liked to cook for hours until the flavor was rich and concentrated, so she settled for buying a few jars of a brand she sometimes used in a pinch. Once she simmered it with some browned sausage, it should be a palatable substitute.

Maddie thoughtfully navigated the aisles, dropping whatever else caught her eye into her cart. She also made sure she grabbed the bread, milk, eggs, and butter no self-respecting kitchen should be without. She was pleasantly surprised to see the small local store, a new addition since Maddie's day, also had its own bakery department, and she brought a loaf of still warm bread to her nose and inhaled the sweet, yeasty scent. It would go perfectly with the pasta dish. She tossed it in the cart. Some fresh salad ingredients, a selection of fruit, a bottle of Italian dressing, and a jug of iced tea, and she had everything she needed for not only dinner but also plenty for the next few days. "I think that's it. That should get me through the week."

Sam had offered to push the cart while she walked ahead and made her selections. More than once, she'd turned suddenly to find his eyes glued to her backside.

"That should get you through the next six months." He eyed the overflowing mound of groceries. "Maybe you *should* have brought those fat pants."

"Not funny, Barstow." Maddie eyed the cart, considering his observation seriously. "Well, maybe I did go a little overboard, but until the car is ready, I wanted to make sure I don't run out of anything. I can't keep expecting you to cart my tail everywhere I need to go if the car is tied up." She would have to find a buyer for the car, too. Eventually. She could never afford to maintain it in the city. The cost of parking alone would be nearly as much as her rent.

Her phone vibrated against her butt cheek. She pulled it free and glanced down at the display, then shoved it back in her pocket.

"You aren't going to answer it? Could be important."

"Nope, definitely not important. Just a persistent pain who doesn't know when to quit."

"If you say so." Sam regarded her for a long moment then turned his attention to a cellophane bag on top of the cart and frowned. "Rice cakes? Ugh, you weren't planning to serve these with dinner, were you? I might have to rethink the plan."

"Suit yourself, but you don't know what you're missing." Maddie winked.

"I'll take my chances. You sure you have everything you need?"

"Yep."

Everything she could buy in a grocery store, anyway.

****

Sam insisted on carrying the bags inside, leaving them on the counter for Maddie to sort through. Maddie wondered if he might kiss her again, but after staring at her intently for a moment, he simply promised to be back at six. After unpacking the bags and putting everything away, she scoured the cupboards until she found a skillet and crumbled the sausage into the pan to brown. She finally found a bowl in the cabinet near the sink that was large enough to put together the cheese filling, but she had to take down a pile of cereal bowls to get to it. Having the bowls near the sink seemed counterproductive. Moving the drinking glasses to the cabinet nearest the sink struck her as eminently more practical. Of course, it left her with a stack of cereal bowls sitting on the counter. Since she needed to make space for them anyway, it seemed perfectly natural to empty all the cupboards and re-organize them according to her own sense of order and logic. After completing the task, she regarded her efforts with a satisfied smile. Then her face fell when she realized what a colossal waste of time the entire endeavor had been. Oh well, at least it was a more workable space for the short time she planned to be here.

She poured the jars of sauce into the pan with the cooked sausage and turned the heat down to simmer. She'd purchased an aluminum lasagna pan at the market since she had no idea what cookware her father did or didn't have. She'd also bought the no-boil lasagna noodles to save time. She ladled some sauce in the pan, put down a layer of the pasta, and smeared it with the cheese mixture. She repeated the layers until the pan was filled, topped it with some grated mozzarella, covered it with foil, and popped it in the oven.

The dish would need to bake for at least an hour, so she decided she might as well take her overnight bag upstairs and see what Sam and her father had done with her room. After the whole backyard fiasco, she hoped it wasn't going to have pink gingham bedding and shelves filled with My Little Pony.

When she reached the top of the stairs, she peeked more closely into the bathroom. Bright and modern, and recently renovated in the same style as the one off the kitchen—albeit, it was larger and had a deep soaking tub in addition to the standup shower. The hallway doubled back on itself with one bedroom next to the bathroom, her father's midway along the hall, and hers at the far end, at the back of the house. Maddie noticed Sam had set her larger bag outside her room. Bypassing the closed doors of the first two, she made her way to the end of the hall. Sucking in a deep breath, she held it, pushed open the door, and stepped inside.

The air left her body in a loud whoosh. The room boasted neither a hint of pink nor a single plastic pony. The walls were a warm, buttery cream, the sumptuous bedding blending various shades of the same hue with brown and gold. The furniture was dark oak in the Mission-style Maddie had always loved and had never been able to afford. A stained glass lamp in a geometric pattern stood on each nightstand, and a flat screen TV perched on top of a chest of drawers facing the bed. A small round table and two armless chairs upholstered in a fawn tone-on-tone striped fabric sat in front of the large window overlooking the backyard.

When she tried to swallow, she found her throat thick and tight. She couldn't fathom how her father would know. The room had been designed and decorated according to every dream she'd ever had of the perfect room. With the window framing the backyard like a mirror into the past, it was an uncanny blend of the child she had been and the woman she had become. The degree of thought that had gone into the room simultaneously stole her breath and broke her heart.

After reverently touching every single thing in the room with trembling hands, she turned back to her luggage with a shaky breath. Reluctant to risk soiling the lovely comforter with her well-used bag, she laid it on the floor instead and tugged the zipper open. She shook out the gauzy broomstick skirt and white silk tank top she planned to don before Sam arrived and spread them on the bed. The skirt's intricate blue and white pattern appealed to her artistic eye and was the closest thing to dressy she'd brought with her. Fortunately, she'd also thought to throw a pair of flat, strappy sandals in her bag since her sneakers wouldn't exactly achieve the fashion statement she hoped for. She unpacked the rest of what little she'd brought and neatly stowed it away. Then she gathered her toiletries together and headed for the bathroom.

As she passed her father's bedroom, the door creaked open of its own accord. Maddie paused as a cool breeze snaked around her ankles causing the hair on the back of her neck to quiver to attention. The seconds ticked by as she held her breath and waited for…she didn't know exactly what she waited for, but whatever it was, nothing further happened. She decided Jeff Hagen probably hadn't closed the door properly when he toured the house earlier. It was ridiculous to imagine it as anything more. She reached for the knob and pulled the door closed with an audible click. Shaking her head at her overactive imagination, she continued down the hall to the bathroom.

She arranged her shampoo and body wash on a shelf in the shower, stowing her toothbrush and toothpaste in the medicine cabinet, and her make-up bag in the vanity drawer. In the closet next to the shower, she found the small stackable washer and dryer Sam had alluded to during the Realtor's visit. The delight she felt at knowing she wouldn't have to drag the meager wardrobe she'd packed to and from a laundromat was directly proportional to the abhorrence she had for laundromats in general. She'd been using one for years and hated every minute of it. It would be a dream to be able to do her laundry without leaving the house.

The mouthwatering aroma of tomato sauce and garlic filled the house as the lasagna baked. Maddie glanced at her watch and saw she still had at least half an hour before it would be time to take the dish out of the oven. Having worked up quite a sweat at Caroline's, she decided to indulge in another shower. She had no illusions dinner with Sam was anything other than payback for his kindness, but that didn't mean she couldn't be fresh.

She went back into the bedroom and quickly stripped. She grabbed a fresh set of white, lacy undies and a matching bra, then reached for her robe and froze. She thought she'd left the framed photograph of her smiling six-year-old self, flanked by her parents, which she never traveled without, on top of her bag. Yet, now it stood propped on the nightstand. She drew in a deep, shaky breath, detecting the faint scent of cherry tobacco, and blew it out again. Of course, she must have put it on the nightstand. She'd been distracted, and it's where she planned to put it. She'd simply forgotten she'd done it. The hair on her arms prickling with awareness, she walked a little more quickly than necessary back down the hall to the bathroom. She needed sleep. Lots and lots of sleep.

It should have been quick work to lather, rinse, and repeat, but she kept remembering that damn kiss. As she ran her hands over her body, she couldn't help imagining Sam Barstow's big, rough hands sliding over her soap-slicked skin. Her toes curled simply thinking about it, and she gave herself a mental shake. What was wrong with her anyway? So what if Sam was as attractive as ever, just as sweet, and had a body to die for? She was here on a temporary basis only, and she was the last person he'd be interested in. As soon as her time was up, she'd make a beeline out of town, hopefully with a signed contract for the house and the promise of a big fat check in her future. She hadn't come here looking for anything or anyone. She stepped under the spray to rinse the soap and her wayward thoughts down the drain.

By the time she climbed out of the shower, dried off, and dressed, it was later than she expected. She settled for dragging a brush through her wet locks, allowing her hair to dry in its natural waves, slipped her feet into the sandals, and hurried down the stairs into the kitchen.

After a five-minute search to locate oven mitts, she tugged the heavy dish from the oven and set it on the stove. The top was brown and crunchy and the cheese bubbled furiously around the edges. Perfect. She turned the oven off, covered the dish with foil, and put the pan back inside to keep it warm until Sam arrived. She quickly washed the dishes she'd used in her meal preparation, then dried and put them away. Tearing open a cellophane bag of mixed field greens, she dumped them into a bowl along with some cherry tomatoes, sliced cucumber, black olives, and feta cheese. She tossed everything together, covered the bowl with plastic wrap, and popped it back in the fridge, deciding she would add the salad dressing when Sam arrived. She despised soggy salad.

Glancing at her watch, she hurried to set the table, placing the serviceable white stoneware plates on two quilted red placemats she'd found in the drawer where the oven mitts had been hiding. She filled the glasses with ice, sliced the bread on a plate, set out the butter and a small dish of grated cheese. She emptied and rinsed the remains of the morning's coffee from the coffeemaker and prepped a fresh pot leaving the machine turned off and ready to brew in case Sam wanted coffee after the meal. Damn! She hadn't thought to get anything for dessert. She had no idea if Sam still had a sweet tooth, but he'd certainly seemed to enjoy Caroline's cake at lunch. Oh well, she did have fruit.

She pulled another bowl down from the cabinet and artistically arranged a couple of apples, pears, and oranges interspersed with red and green grapes. It would have to do. She plunked it down in the center of the table deciding it actually made quite an attractive centerpiece as well. Wired with nervous energy and ready to jump out of her skin, she rearranged the fruit three times. She reminded herself to breathe. This wasn't an actual date or anything. With everything in place, she wandered out to the front porch and settled herself in the porch swing. At last, she had a few minutes to sit and relax.

Chapter Six

Sam swung the truck into his driveway and clicked off the ignition, completely annoyed at the idiotic grin that kept tugging at his lips since he dropped Maddie at her place. The smile dimmed when he realized she didn't consider it her place anymore, she considered it her father's place, and she wasn't planning to stay. He'd been in a nearly constant state of arousal for most of the day, and he craved a cold shower and the time to get his erratic thoughts in some kind of order before he saw her again. So far, he hadn't detected a glimpse of the heartless bitch he'd been expecting. Maybe it would be easier if he had. Whatever her reasons for leaving without a word, even if she'd never given *him* a second thought, seeing her reactions today, he realized the separation from her father hadn't been any easier for her than it had been for Frank. He also saw the way she'd jumped in to help Caroline, and there sure as hell hadn't been anything in it for her. Self-centered people simply didn't do things like that. Having spent half her life trying to earn acceptance, she probably wasn't used to people accepting her at face value. But people did here. It had been one of the main reasons he'd decided to settle in the small cottage where he'd spent summers with his maternal grandmother instead of at the family compound in Greeley. No one here wasted time banging his head against the brick wall of his mistakes.

They accepted him for who he was instead of who they thought he should be. He climbed stiffly from the car absently massaging his bum knee. These days it was a nervous habit more than any sense of actual discomfort. The physical pain ended a long time ago.

Sam had never expected Maddie still would be a woman he could fall for. Hell, he was afraid he might already be halfway gone, if he'd ever gotten over her at all. Since Teresa walked out, he'd avoided anything that threatened to be more than a casual fling like a communicable disease. Now he found himself fantasizing about a woman who'd already tossed him aside like a half-eaten sandwich and walked away without any explanation. He'd have to be a complete and utter fool to take a stroll down that path again, no matter how tempting he found her. The sooner her house sold the better.

Sam unlocked the door and let the peace he always felt upon entering the place soak into his bones. His grandmother's cottage sat along the shore of a small lake about ten minutes outside town. A grove of evergreens, which had inspired the town's name over two hundred years before, surrounded the lake. Pine Lake was too small and shallow to accommodate watersports, and in Sam's opinion, it was the major part of its appeal. It remained quiet, unspoiled, and private while lakes in the surrounding areas contended with soaring real estate prices, homes built as status symbols instead of family retreats, and ongoing competitions to see who had the biggest and fastest water toys.

The place had originally been constructed for summer use, and Sam had expended a good deal of financial and sweat equity to winterize and renovate it.

He'd opened up the main floor so that standing at the front door, he could see straight through to a spectacular view of the sun glinting off the lake through the large glass doors leading from the kitchen to the deck. The one piece of his father's advice Sam had actually paid attention to was to hire a financial advisor who made sure Sam didn't squander the trust fund from his grandmother or the obscenely high salary he received for the few short years of his career. Though he could live quite comfortably on his savings and investments if he chose, he kept busy doing odd jobs, preferring to live simply—just one more bone of contention between himself and the rest of his extravagant family.

He tossed his keys on the kitchen counter and noticed the red light flashing on the answering machine. He checked the caller ID and his gut tightened.

"Sonofabitch. What the hell does he want?"

He hadn't heard from his father in months, and that was precisely the way he liked it. In the Barstow household, there were only two ways to do anything. His father's way and the wrong way. Sam had been bucking the old man for most of his life. First, he'd had the poor sense to fall in love with a girl from the wrong social sphere, then he'd gone into the security business instead of assuming his reserved role in the revered family empire. Edward Barstow never made any attempt to conceal his disappointment in his eldest son's choices and was the first to say I told you so when everything went south. For a while, Sam bought into it, doubted himself, wondered if maybe his father had been right about him all along. But once he got his head together, with the help of good friends like Frank, Sam realized the choices he'd made were the right ones for him. He wasn't obligated to live up to anyone's expectations except his own. Still, his father was a persistent, intimidating sonofabitch who believed he could eventually humiliate Sam into shouldering the burden of Barstow Enterprises if he kept badgering him long enough. Sam knew the boardroom better suited his younger brother Rob, and suspected his father knew it, too. But it made no difference to Edward Barstow. For him, everything was about control. It always had been. Intellectually, Sam knew all this, but every time he talked to his father, his muscles coiled into knots and he began a slow descent down a slippery slope leading to the abyss of self-doubt. He wasn't about to return his father's call and end up in *that* mood tonight.

He peeled his shirt over his head and wadded it into a ball. After scoring a two point shot in the laundry basket sitting outside the bathroom door, he pulled off his boots and removed his belt. His jeans followed the shirt. He strode into the bathroom and cranked on the shower. The thing was huge, a masterpiece of marble, chrome, and glass large enough to host a small party. Two fourteen inch rain heads mimicked the luxurious drenching of a summer downpour while a variety of fifty-four-nozzle body sprays provided concurrent gentle spray and targeted hydro-massage coming at him from every direction. Sam turned his face into the jets. The setup cost a small fortune and was his one indulgence. The damn thing almost rivaled sex. He thought of Maddie. Imagined her slick, wet, and hot…for him. Pictured her face as she…

Sam yanked the faucet to the right with a groan as the water turned to ice. Okay, maybe the shower couldn't quite compete.

In less than ten minutes, Sam found himself standing in front of his open closet briskly rubbing his chest with a towel. He rifled through his clothes for the third time. It annoyed him to no end to realize he was acting like a goddamn girl. It was a simple dinner, for God's sake. With a muffled curse, he yanked a pair of jeans and a simple, button-down oxford from their hangers and pulled them on. He rolled the sleeves back over his forearms, the crisp white shirt contrasting sharply with his deeply tanned skin and straining tautly across his shoulders and chest as he bent to jerk his boots on. Shoving his wallet and cell phone in his pocket, he headed out the door.

****

Maddie kicked off her shoes and tucked one foot beneath her, using the other to push against the porch deck and rock the swing lazily back and forth. She reflected on how quiet and peaceful it was—no traffic, no crowds, no sirens—nothing but birdsong and the faint squeak of the swing to disturb the silence. No sooner had the thought crossed her mind than she discerned the feeble sound of someone calling out. She planted her foot on the porch to stop the swing and cocked her head, listening. The call came again, followed closely by a dull, metallic rapping that seemed to be coming from the neighbor's front door. Maddie slipped her sandals back on, rose from the swing, and headed down the steps. As she cautiously approached the neighbor's porch, she realized the rapping indeed came from inside. She crept up to the storm door and nervously peeked in. An elderly woman lay on the floor inside, the end of her cane against the bottom of the aluminum door, and her lined face pale and contorted.

"Thank God," the woman gasped with a pained grimace. "Been calling and banging for an hour hoping someone would pass by and hear me. Couldn't reach the phone."

"Mrs. Evans? Oh gosh, what happened?" Maddie automatically reached for her phone and realized she'd left it in the house.

"Maddie Moran? Well, butter my butt and call me a biscuit! When did you get home? Seems I've fallen, and I can't get up!" The old woman started to laugh at her own feeble joke, but it quickly deteriorated into a moan of pain. "Think maybe I broke something."

Through the door, Maddie noticed the woman's left leg seemed shorter and pulled toward the middle of her body at an awkward angle. She bet her neighbor was right. She maybe broke something, maybe a hip, by the looks of it. Maddie didn't see any way she could get in without risking further damage as the woman had fallen with her body wedged against the door. She said as much as she started to back away intending to head next door for her phone.

"No! Please...don't leave me. The back door is open, just come right through," her neighbor gasped.

Maddie pressed her lips together as she made her way to the back of the house. Where she came from, no one would ever have left the door unlocked. Maddie vaguely remembered the house had the same basic layout as hers, though it wasn't nearly as modern, and photos and knick-knacks cluttered every conceivable surface. There were starched doilies everywhere; including the backs and arms of the living room chairs. The faded scent of old roses and mothballs tickled her nostrils as she navigated her way to the front door. She cried out in alarm when she found the woman struggling to lever herself into a sitting position.

"Stay right there and don't move," Maddie called, her heart pounding. She was no expert when it came to emergencies, but she did know you weren't supposed to move people if they had an accident. She figured that went for people moving themselves, too. "Where's the phone?"

The woman pointed to a small table near the stairs, and Maddie put in a call to 9-1-1. After providing the address and what little information she could, the dispatcher assured her the paramedics were on their way.

"I got in last night," she offered after returning to the woman and kneeling beside her on the floor. "I'll only be staying until the house sells."

"I'm sorry to hear that." The woman bit her lip in pain and clawed at Maddie's hand. "It's a shame we couldn't meet again under better circumstances. I'm so sorry about your father...such a nice man. Kept my grass cut and all that kind of stuff when I couldn't do it anymore. Would never take a penny from me, either."

"Oh, um, thank you," Maddie replied automatically. She felt as though she should be doing something while they waited for the ambulance to arrive, but hadn't the faintest idea what that something might be. "Is there someone I can call for you?"

"Well, I guess my daughter Diane will have to know." Mrs. Evans frowned. "This will be just one more bullet in her gun."

"Excuse me?" Maddie opened her eyes wide in confusion.

"She's never happy unless she's treating me like a helpless two-year-old," Mrs. Evans grumbled. "She thinks I'm too old and feeble to live here alone. Wants me to sell the place and move in with her. Don't get me wrong, I love my grandkids, and would be happy to see more of them, but I'm not ready to be put out to pasture, yet. Don't you start treating me like an old woman, too," she snapped as Maddie grabbed a pillow from the sofa and stuck it under her head.

"Mrs. Evans, I hate to be the one to break it to you, but you *are* kind of an old woman. Not that it makes you helpless, but I suspect it *does* make you a little stubborn," Maddie replied with a tolerant smile while calmly dialing the number the woman had given for her daughter. Maddie remembered the girl only vaguely. Diane had been several years older, and even though they lived next door to one another, they had a completely different circle of friends. "I'm sure it's not that she thinks you're helpless. She loves you and probably just worries about you here by yourself."

By the time she explained who she was, what had happened, and calmed Diane down enough to listen to reason, Maddie found she'd agreed to ride with Hannah Evans in the ambulance to the hospital. She'd also promised to stay with her until Diane could find a babysitter and get there from her place, at least thirty minutes away. As soon as Maddie completed the call and returned to Hannah's side, the frightened woman's thin fingers reached for her, clutching at her hand like a lifeline. Maddie hadn't had anyone depend on her in a long time, and it was a little unnerving, but kind of nice in a way, too. And Frank *had* cut the woman's grass. So although technically they were strangers after all these years, they kind of weren't. At least that's how Maddie decided to spin it. Her heart sank as she realized she couldn't even call Sam to let him know what was going on since she didn't have his number. It was already after five thirty. She would never get back in time.

As soon as the ambulance arrived, Maddie excused herself after making the attendants promise they would wait for her. She ran next door and grabbed her phone and her purse. She had no idea how long this might take, but assumed she would be able to get a cab home. Scribbling a quick note to Sam, she left the warm lasagna in the oven, flicked on the porch light anticipating it would be dark when she got back, and stuck the note to the front door on her way out.

****

Sam turned the nose of his truck into Maddie's driveway promptly thirty minutes later. He'd given himself quite a lecture on the way over. Bottom line, they'd been two young, inexperienced kids who'd confused lust with love. Yep, he was going to go with that. He would do what he could to help Maddie while she was here, ensure she got a fair price for the house, and wave good-bye with no regrets when she went back to her life. It was what she said she wanted, and all things considered, it was probably for the best. The more he thought about it, the more he questioned Frank's real motive in extracting Sam's promise to watch out for Maddie. No matter how much affection and respect he'd had for Frank Moran, he had no intention of allowing a dead man to play posthumous cupid and dupe him into a doomed relationship. It was physical attraction, plain and simple. Probably. Maybe he should just take her to bed and get her the hell out of

81

his system.

Although it was barely dusk, Sam noticed the porch light glowing as soon as he loped up the steps. The folded paper taped to the front door with his name on it caught his attention next.

Sam,
Gone to hospital. Don't know how long I'll be.
Lasagna in the oven, salad in fridge.
Please help yourself.
Sorry.
M.

His mouth went oddly dry, and his heart skipped a beat as he read the note. *What the hell?* Sam crumpled the paper and let it fall to the porch deck. He dug the key out of his pocket and let himself in. Heart in his throat, he quickly checked for any telltale sign of what might have happened. Nothing. In fact, everything seemed in remarkably good order. Ignoring the instinctual reaction of his grumbling stomach to the scent of the lasagna, his mind raced as he tried to figure out what could have sent her to the hospital. Maybe she had some chronic health problem he didn't know about? He checked to make sure the oven was off, then yanked open the cabinet to grab a quick glass of water before heading out. There were cereal bowls where the glasses should have been. He finally found what he was looking for after a systematic inspection of the cabinets. She'd rearranged the kitchen?

He gulped down the drink and raced out to the truck, sending gravel flying in every direction as he peeled out and sped off in the direction of Pine Grove Memorial. He didn't stop to analyze the unreasonable panic he felt at the thought of something happening to

Maddie Moran. She was a virtual stranger in town, maybe hurt and alone. She had to be scared to death. He would be just as concerned about anyone under the circumstances. Of course, he would.

Ignoring the Emergency Vehicles Only sign, he screeched into a parking space in record time, slammed the gearshift into park, and threw open the door almost before the vehicle had come to a complete stop. He didn't have the patience to wait for the automatic doors, which, in Sam's opinion, moved far too slowly for a place claiming to deal in emergencies. He pushed against the frame with either hand and forced the heavy glass and metal slabs apart more quickly by wedging his large body in between them. The doors protested with a high pitched squeal that caught the attention of the bored-looking desk clerk sitting behind a window inside. Sam planted his palms on the counter and leaned down to speak into the round hole cut into the glass.

"Hi, I'm looking for Madigan Moran."

The young brunette cracked her gum and regarded him over a pair of rhinestone-studded, leopard-patterned glasses. Her heavily mascaraed lashes flicked up and down, tangling like spider's legs, as she conspicuously gave him the once-over and apparently decided she liked what she saw.

"Are you a family member?" She smiled brightly with her short, black lacquered nails poised over the computer keyboard.

"Does it matter?" Sam returned her smile with a forced one of his own. The kid couldn't have been more than eighteen, and though Sam was out of practice, he hadn't forgotten how to turn on the charm where women were concerned.

"Well." She swallowed hard and her tongue snaked out to wet her lips in a gesture she probably believed was provocative. "I'm not supposed to give out any information. HIPAA absolutely forbids it," she announced in a well-rehearsed tone. "Patient privacy and all, ya know? I could lose my job."

"I see," Sam drawled with a wink. "Well, I sure don't want to be the reason you lose your job. Let's just say I'm her brother Sam, okay?"

"Um, okay," the teenager giggled. "Why don't you have a seat over there, brother Sam, and I'll see what I can find out?" She rose from the chair and disappeared into the back, her hips swaying in such an exaggerated manner that Sam knew it was for his benefit. Maybe he'd laid it on a little thick considering she was just a kid. Of course, it'd worked, so maybe he shouldn't complain. He would have news about Madigan any minute.

Sam crammed his large frame into one of the molded plastic and chrome chairs attached to the wall with bolts and screws. The waiting room was nearly empty. A young mother sat in one corner with an infant next to her in a child seat on the floor, and a flushed toddler curled miserably in her lap. A leather-clad octogenarian with drooping tattoos sat nursing a grotesquely swollen hand in another. Aside from them, the outdated television on the wall played to an empty room. Must be a slow night in Pine Grove, Sam mused. Then again, it usually was. It was one of the things he loved about it.

"Sam?" Little Miss Leopard Specs motioned him over to the window. Sam jumped out of the chair in a flash.

"Listen," she whispered glancing around to make sure no one would overhear. "I checked all the holding beds and all of the current charts…your, um, sister isn't registered."

"What?" Sam stared blankly. "She has to be here. Pine Grove Memorial is the only hospital within twenty miles. Could she have been admitted? Or transferred out to another hospital?" Which would mean that whatever happened had been too serious to treat here. The bottom dropped out of Sam's stomach.

"No." The teen shook her head. "She'd still appear in the system. There's no record of anyone by that name having been here, at all."

"Well, uh, thanks." Sam squinted at her hospital issued name badge. "Sherrie. I appreciate you checking."

"Anytime, Sam." She gave him a come-hither smile that would probably have been a lot more effective without the braces. "I work every Tuesday, Thursday, and Saturday. I get off at eleven if you're, um, ever in the neighborhood." Sam wondered how she managed to bat her lashes at that speed weighted down as they were with a pound of make-up. A cute kid probably hid under all the war paint.

"Kind of late to be working on a school night, isn't it?"

"Well, yeah, but…" A warm, red stain suffused her face as she realized she taken the bait. "Well, I'll be eighteen in a couple months," she muttered miserably.

"Well, you have a happy birthday in case I don't see you, Sherrie…and thanks, again. I really appreciate the help." Sam winked and flashed his dimple. "Don't work too hard. Bye."

"Bye." A resigned sigh escaped her lips. She shoved her glasses up the bridge of her nose and offered him a tinsel-shiny grin. "Hope you find your *sister*."

"Thanks," Sam called absently over his shoulder. "Me too." He shouldered his way back through the automatic doors into the rapidly darkening evening. Where in the hell could she be?

Chapter Seven

The woman kept her head down as she hurried toward the entrance, and she barreled into Sam's chest before the doors had even swished closed behind him. He shot out a hand to steady her, and her head shot up with a quick, indrawn breath and a half formed apology on her lips. When she saw him, her face creased into a relieved smile.

"Sorry…Sam! What are you doing here? I hope everything's okay?"

"Hey, Diane. Yeah, I'm good, but what about you? Not one of the kids, I hope?"

"No, thank God, though not for lack of trying on their part." She laughed tiredly. "No, my mom fell and broke her hip. At least I think she did. I won't be sure until I talk to the doctors. I feel terrible it took me so long to get here. I couldn't get hold of my husband and had to wait until he got home to stay with the kids. I'm sure by this time that poor woman is probably really sorry she got involved!"

"Woman?" Sam's heart rate tripped and steadied as the light bulb came on. It continued to decrease, reaching an almost normal rhythm, as Diane continued.

"Yes, Frank Moran's daughter, Maddie. Oh, heck, what am I thinking? You know her, of course. You guys were in the same class, right?" Diane smiled, but it didn't erase the drawn expression on her face. "She heard Mom calling for help and took care of everything. She even offered to stay with her until I could get here. Wasn't that nice of her? She's a lot like Frank, I guess."

"Yeah, she's a nice girl," Sam agreed, privately hoping Diane kept the comparison to Frank to herself when she saw Maddie. Yeah, she was a nice girl. A nice girl who could have been a little more explicit in her note. Then again, she couldn't have anticipated he would jump to the wrong conclusion and get all bent out of shape worrying about her. Hell, he hadn't known it himself.

"Well, you'd better get in there and check on your mom. I hope everything's okay. Tell Madigan I'm here to give her a ride home, will you?"

"What? Oh, sure. I'll tell her. Nice to see you, Sam."

"You too, Diane. Give Hannah my best."

"You bet, right after I read her the riot act." Diane sighed. "Maybe this will finally convince her to sell the place and move in with us. I didn't worry as much when Frank was alive. He'd check on her at least once a day, but now that his house is empty...well, I'm just thankful his daughter was there. Otherwise, Mom could have been lying there alone and in pain until tomorrow when I came over." Moisture gathered in her eyes.

"No sense upsetting yourself over what could have happened, Diane. It didn't. Maddie *was* there, and your mom is a tough old bird. She'll do fine," Sam encouraged. "Now go on and get in there. She's probably giving the doctors fits."

"She probably is," Diane agreed with a watery smile. "Thanks, Sam. I'll send Madigan out."

They headed back inside. Diane went straight to

Sherrie's little window and immediately disappeared into the back as soon as she gave her name. Sam decided to forego the dubious comfort of the plastic chair and settled for leaning back against the wall with his arms crossed over his chest and his eyes fixed on the door to the treatment area.

He didn't have long to wait. Madigan came rushing out with her cell phone plastered to her ear. She stopped dead when she saw him there waiting, and held up a finger. A worried frown creased her smooth brow and her face was pale and drawn.

"Of course you're upset, Chris. I'm upset too, and I'm not even there. But you don't think they took anything else? What did the police say?" She crossed to stand in front of Sam listening intently. "Well, call the locksmith…no…call right now. I sold a painting last week. I can cover it, and you can pay me back your half when you get it. Or put it toward my rent. Text me your account information, and I'll transfer the money over when I get home."

The phone bleeped and Maddie pulled it away from her ear to check the display.

"Okay, got it. Yes, of course I'll delete it once I transfer the money. I'm not the brightest bulb in the chandelier, but I'm not a moron, either." Maddie rolled her eyes. "Get the locks changed on the door, and get the one on the kitchen window fixed. Do it tonight. Text me the total, and I'll transfer the money. Just write the guy a check. The money will be there by the time he's able to cash it. What? Ian? When? What in the hell did he want? You didn't let him in, did you?" Maddie listened for a few minutes more, and then clicked off the call with a heavy sigh after reminding the person on the other end to send the total for the locksmith. She raised her remarkable green eyes with a weary smile.

"Thanks for coming, Sam. Even your dirty old truck is preferable to a cab. Whew! It has been one hell of a day, and I sure hadn't planned on *that* call to top it off."

"No problem," Sam replied easily. "I gather it wasn't good news?" He draped an arm over her shoulders to steer her toward the exit. It was completely dark outside, but the entrance was well lit and Sam had parked his truck nearby, so they didn't have far to go.

"That was my roommate, Chris. When she got home from work, she found the lock jimmied and everything in the apartment trashed, including my studio. Also known as the corner of my bedroom. She doesn't think there's anything missing, other than a coffee can filled with loose change that we left out on the counter in plain sight, but it really shook her. Doesn't do a whole lot for my nerves, either." Maddie gave a wobbly laugh. "We've never had any trouble before. It's kind of a quiet neighborhood usually."

"What do the police say?" Sam asked.

Maddie shrugged. "What could they say? They made a report, advised her to change the locks, and promised they'd get back to her with any new developments. Probably kids hoping for quick cash."

"And she's sure nothing else is missing?" Sam held the door open, and Maddie climbed in and settled into the seat with a weary groan. She leaned her head back and closed her eyes. She thought yesterday had been a long day, but today certainly led the competition for top spot. Sam and the lamp incident, the yard, and an unexpected grief for her father had already pushed the limits of what she could absorb in a twenty-four hour period. Only a glutton would then promise to help out at the diner, spend hours at the hospital with an injured neighbor, and contend with a break-in. So much for the peace and serenity of small town life she'd looked forward to.

"Nothing that she could tell," Maddie confirmed when Sam had climbed in the driver's side and started the engine. "It's not like either of us have much of value. I have a couple pieces of my mother's jewelry I suppose might be worth something, but I have them with me. So other than some outdated television and stereo equipment, it's pretty slim pickings in our little corner of the world."

"Give me your phone," he demanded with an outstretched palm. Maddie handed it over with a puzzled frown and watched while Sam entered his number and saved it in her contacts. Then he checked her number and entered it into his phone before dropping his in his shirt pocket and handing hers back.

"There. Next time you run into a problem, you'll be able to call someone. Well, at least neither of you were home at the time. There were a couple break-ins last week in Greeley. Both were women living on their own. The cops didn't make much of it since they didn't take anything except some lingerie. Still, people have died for less than lingerie or some outdated television and stereo equipment just by being in the wrong place at the wrong time."

"Yeah, I guess so." Maddie covered her mouth as a jaw-cracking yawn snuck up and caught her by surprise. With a faint smile at his unexpected thoughtfulness, she tucked her phone back into her purse.

"So, who's Ian?" He really hadn't intended to ask, his tongue simply had a moment of independence from his brain.

"No one important. How was the lasagna?"

"What? Oh, beats me," Sam replied. "I got your note and headed over here. I, uh, thought maybe you got hurt or something."

"I guess I should have been a little more specific. Sorry about that. I didn't want to leave Hannah alone for any length of time. The poor thing was scared to death. And thanks again for coming for me. This is much better than a cab ride."

"No problem." Sam smiled without taking his eyes from the road. The traffic increased as they got closer to downtown, and Maddie straightened in her seat gazing around curiously. For a small town, there certainly was a lot of activity. Shops, cafes, and restaurants all appeared to be open and small knots of people were gathered near the entrances and seated at small outdoor tables. Families hung out on the benches in the square and mothers kept a careful eye on small children playing near the fountain. Maddie wouldn't have believed such a charming scene still existed, in this day and age.

"It's still so nice here," she said thoughtfully, surprised at the wistful note that crept into her voice. "It's just remained kind of old school and unspoiled."

"There's a new mall about five miles outside town with one of those big movie complexes. The kids gravitate there these days, but yeah, overall Pine Grove is still kind of wholesome and old-fashioned, I guess." Sam shrugged. "Everyone knows almost everyone else.

Of course, the downside is everyone knows almost everyone else."

"Why is that a downside?" Maddie asked.

"Because it means everyone also knows everyone else's business." Sam grinned. "Forgot what you did last week? Just ask the neighbor."

"Oh, really?" Maddie drawled with a slow smile. "And what could they tell me about you, Sam Barstow?" Maddie turned in the seat to face him, but he didn't even glance her way as he spoke.

"More than I'd like probably." He hit the brakes harder than necessary as the light turned red. Maddie's neck snapped back and forth from the jolt. "Just make sure you're prepared for the answers before you start asking the questions."

"You've never struck me as the kind of man that has much to hide."

"Everyone has something to hide. I'm no different than anyone else."

"I see. And if I asked what it is you're hiding…would you tell me?"

Sam's jaw tightened imperceptibly. "Yes."

"You would?"

"Yep." He let out the clutch and started through the intersection as the light changed to green. "I'm sure as hell not a saint, Maddie, but I do try to at least be honest."

"Well, that's good to know," Maddie replied slowly. "Anyway, if you were as perfect as you seem…well, I'm not sure I'd actually believe it anyway."

"Nobody's perfect, least of all me, so don't hang that albatross around my neck. You'll only be disappointed." His knuckles were white where he gripped the steering wheel. "If there's something you want to know, ask."

"Okay…why aren't you married?" That seemed like a good place to start. He was damned attractive, sweet, and thoughtful, in short, he was quite a catch. She knew it better than anyone. It seemed strange some woman wouldn't have scooped him up by now.

"I was. I'm not anymore."

"Oh." *Open mouth, insert foot, Moran.* She carefully withdrew her toes from her throat and coughed to clear it. "I'm, uh, sorry."

His teeth flashed white in the dim illumination of the dash lights. "Thanks, but don't be. We're both happier now. Teresa was a bright nights, big city kind of girl. She hated Pine Grove, almost as much as she hated being saddled with a husband who refused to move in the circles of wealth and celebrity. She married me expecting a certain lifestyle. Turned out she was more attracted to the lifestyle than the man. The things that were important to her just weren't important to me, and she got out."

"She was a fool. That sucks, Sam. I really am sorry. It must have been painful for you."

"Wasn't the first time a woman walked out on me."

She couldn't miss the way his jaw tightened. Or the implication. She had no business judging his ex when she'd walked out on him, too. He didn't say anything further, and his eyes remained glued to the road.

"You're right," she whispered at last. "It's none of my business. I was out of line."

"Well, we were introduced by my father, and the two of them were thick as thieves. Guess that should have been my first clue." Sam smiled again. "The man is nothing if not determined."

Sam pulled into Maddie's drive, clicked off the engine, and cut the lights, plunging them into nearly total darkness. He stared straight ahead. Then he rubbed the back of his neck, cleared his throat, and turned to face her.

"Listen, there's something I need to say. I didn't plan to tell you this, but I decided you should hear it from me before you heard it from someone else. I hadn't planned on retiring, Madigan."

"Oh, I just assumed—"

"Yeah, I figured you did. The truth is, in that line of work, instincts are everything. Mine failed, and it cost lives. I didn't handle it very well. By the time my injuries healed enough to consider going back, I realized security work and the drinking couldn't safely co-exist."

Maddie went very still. Drinking. It didn't seem to imply he'd had one single lapse in judgment. And it would sure as hell explain what he and her father had in common.

"So you're telling me..." Her throat closed. She couldn't force another word through her stiff lips. Even her chest felt tight, as though all the air had been sucked out of the truck cab.

"I'm telling you I had a problem. I tried to drown the guilt in a bottle, but discovered it didn't help in the long run and only created its own set of problems. I haven't touched a drink in over six years. I like to think I'm a different man now, but considering your history...well, I thought you should know."

Maddie's fingers curled into fists until her nails bit

painfully into the soft flesh of her palms. She wanted to punch Sam Barstow square in the forehead. Hard. Of all the sins he could have owned up to, this was the one she was guaranteed to struggle with most. And he knew it. She resisted her first instinct to get out of the truck, run into the house, and slam the door—right after making it clear she never wanted to see his face again. Because it would be a lie. She did want to see his face again, probably a lot more than she should. She'd never really gotten over him. She knew it now. She'd been living her life, but she'd never moved on. But clearly he had, and maybe that was exactly why he'd told her. Some kind of warped poetic justice? She felt his gaze on her as the part of her that feared the disease warred with the part of her beginning to understand people made mistakes but those mistakes didn't have to define them. Her father had made mistakes. Giant, life changing, hurtful mistakes. But he'd acknowledged them and tried to turn his life around, tried to make amends for the pain he'd caused. She'd refused to accept his overtures, but it didn't make them any less sincere.

"Aren't you going to say anything?" His voice told her he'd already anticipated her response. After all, she'd refused to forgive the disease in her own father. Why would she overlook it for him? *People who live in glass houses shouldn't throw stones.* It had been one of her father's favorite sayings, and she hadn't thought of it in years. It seemed particularly appropriate at the moment. Maybe this wasn't simply a question of giving Sam a chance, maybe this was some kind of karmic test. He didn't have to tell her, yet he had. Why? Why not continue the façade until she left? Maddie closed her eyes and swallowed hard. Then she made her decision. It might be the wrong decision. It might not be the smart decision. But if destiny intended she suffer more regrets, she didn't want them to be because she was afraid to stop dribbling and take the shot. Again.

"Yes, Sam. I am going to say something," she began quietly and saw his posture stiffen as though he braced for a physical blow. She reached for the handle and yanked open the door. Sliding from the truck to the ground, she held her skirt so it didn't ride up, and prayed her shaking legs would hold her. "I can't possibly eat all that lasagna myself. Are you coming in?"

****

Sam sat staring through the windshield for several long and painful heartbeats after Maddie's door slammed shut. He must have misheard. He'd fully expected she'd tell him to hit the road. Maybe it was even part of the reason he'd told her the truth. He wouldn't have to fight this attraction if she wouldn't give him the time of day, right? The fact that she didn't reject him when every instinct she had must be screaming at her to run? He might not be the most articulate man and he couldn't have verbalized the way it made him feel, but *good* hardly seemed to cut it. That in itself worried him. He shouldn't give a flying fig what Madigan Moran thought of him. Not anymore. She wasn't here to stay, and he wasn't interested in someone who was. Maddie reached the bottom of the porch steps and turned back toward the truck. If he had half a brain, he'd slam his gearshift into reverse and get the hell out. Now. The porch fixture cast just enough light for him to see her arched brow. Clearly she

97

repeated the invitation without words and waited to see if he would accept. Damn. Silently calling himself every kind of fool, he turned off the truck and opened the door.

When he finally got out of the truck, Maddie started up the steps, digging in her purse for the key. She tugged open the storm door, but as she moved the lock-box aside to fit the key in the lock, the porch light flickered and she hesitated.

"Sam," she asked over her shoulder. "When you stopped by earlier, were you in the house?"

"Yeah," he replied squinting at the light fixture as he reached the top of the steps. "Remind me to check that fixture. Why?"

"Did you lock the door on your way out?"

****

"Of course." He pushed at the door with his index finger, and it creaked open with no resistance at all. He reached inside and clicked on the hall light. "Well, I was in a hurry, maybe I didn't pull it closed all the way. It's probably nothing, but stay here until I have a look."

Maddie dug into her bag, raising her hand triumphantly with her fingers closed around a slim canister of pepper spray. "Like I told you earlier, a girl can never be too careful." She grinned.

"That shit is painful. Guess I should be glad you chose the lamp. Stay here."

Maddie waited on the porch while Sam went through the house flicking on every light as he did. Finally, he came back to the door.

"Nothing seems out of place. I guess I didn't pull it closed when I left. Sorry about that."

"Some executive protector you are! Kidding,"

Maddie added quickly when he stiffened and his brows drew together. "No big deal. I'm just glad you're here. If I'd taken a cab home and found the door open, I probably would have slept on the porch. Come on in and sit down. I'm going to put the lasagna back in the oven for a couple minutes to warm. If you wouldn't mind tossing the salad while I run next door and feed Hannah's cat, we should be able to eat in about twenty minutes."

"You're cat sitting?" Sam couldn't keep the amused tone from his voice.

"Not exactly *sitting*. I can't bring him over here unless I want to spend the foreseeable future with my eyes swollen shut. I guess you forgot I'm allergic to cats," Maddie explained. "But I kind of promised Hannah I would at least check to see he had food and water every day until she got home so Diane wouldn't have to run all the way over here."

"Tell you what. I think you've done your share of good deeds for the day. How about I run over and feed the cat while you heat the lasagna and toss the salad?"

"You wouldn't mind?" Maddie breathed gratefully.

"Not in the least," Sam replied taking the key from her fingers and heading for the back door. He stuck his head back in before he closed it. "And Maddie? Just for the record, I haven't forgotten one damn thing."

****

Maddie stared at the door for several minutes after his cryptic pronouncement. Should she interpret it as a good thing? Or his way of reminding her he hadn't forgiven her for leaving without a word? Hands trembling, she turned the oven to the warm setting and pulled the salad out of the fridge. She added the dressing and gave it a quick toss, then put it in the middle of the table she'd set earlier. The ice had melted in the glasses so she dumped them out and replaced it. She'd covered the bread with plastic wrap and a quick check confirmed it was still soft and fresh. Finally, she poured what remained of the sauce from the jar into a small bowl and put it in the microwave, worried the lasagna might have started to dry out and would need a little extra. Grabbing her purse from the kitchen chair, she took it into the living room intending to deposit it next to the sofa. Then she spied her laptop on the coffee table.

Not such a big deal except that she'd left it upstairs. The bag slipped from her fingers and the contents spilled across the floor. The screen cast an eerie blue glow, and a message scrolled repeatedly across the bright blue monitor. A message clearly meant for her.

Maddie heard Sam pounding up the porch steps seconds after she screamed his name. He burst through the front door as though expecting anything. Maddie stood frozen in place near the sofa, and Sam strode quickly to her side.

She knew he'd arrived, but still jumped when he touched her shoulder. She turned and buried her face against his chest. His arms came around her without hesitation.

"What happened?" He grasped her shoulders and pulled away enough to see her face. Her breath came in rapid little gasps and though her lips moved, she made no sound.

She shook her head mutely.

"What?"

Finally, she brought her arm up and pointed in the direction of the coffee table. Sam tucked her beneath his shoulder and kept her tight against him as he stepped closer to see. She felt him stiffen against her when he focused in on the screen.

Peekaboo, Madigan. I found you.

A series of emoticon smiley faces followed the text as it snaked across the screen repeating itself over and over.

"Shit!" Sam hissed between clenched jaws.

Maddie whispered through stiff lips. "I left my laptop upstairs when I went to the hospital."

"Damn it, I knew I locked that door!" he muttered, forking a hand through his short hair and spiking it in every direction.

"Whether you did or didn't doesn't seem all that important at the moment. Whether someone walked in or broke in, I can count the number of people in this town who even know I'm back on one hand. I can't believe any of them would have done this."

"Trust me, Maddie, This isn't Caroline or Hannah's style. If you left your laptop upstairs, whoever it was had to have gone through the house," Sam reasoned slowly. "Even a stranger could have found your name any number of places…papers in your father's room, luggage tags…"

"My luggage does have identification on it." Maddie breathed a small sigh of relief. "Maybe the message is someone's idea of a bad joke."

"Maybe. Didn't you say you had some of your mother's jewelry with you? Where is it? We should check to make sure nothing is missing, and then I'm calling the cops."

"It's upstairs in a drawer. I know you probably checked the bedroom already, but would you mind coming with me?" Maddie asked in an unsteady voice.

"I'm right behind you," Sam assured her as he pulled his phone from his shirt pocket and punched at the numbers.

He stayed right on Maddie's heels, providing the information to the dispatcher, as she made her way down the hall to her room and flicked on the light. Everything seemed exactly the way she'd left it, but a sickening nausea rolled in the pit of her stomach. Someone had been in here. Someone had gone through her belongings, touched her things. She felt violated and exposed. She crossed the room and opened the dresser drawer where she'd stashed her mother's jewelry.

"Well, damn," Maddie whispered. Her stomach churned like the heavy-duty cycle of a washing machine. Sam clicked the phone off and stepped over to her side.

"The jewelry's gone?" He sighed in a resigned voice. Maddie pulled a small velvet pouch from the drawer and held it aloft for his inspection.

"No, the jewelry is right where I left it." She stared at the drawer then turned to him with wide, worried eyes. "Someone broke in, went through the house, and didn't take a thing, but they took the time to leave that message. Why?"

Chapter Eight

"That might be the best lasagna I've ever tasted. And I'm not even saying that because I missed dinner and could happily have gnawed on the chair leg. Don't suppose you'd share your recipe with my wife?"

Bill Jessup leaned back in his chair and patted his stomach. Maddie lifted another hefty cut of lasagna onto the spatula and held it toward him. He held up a hand to refuse. Sam crooked a finger toward his plate to indicate he was ready for seconds. Or was it thirds? At any rate, she was just happy to see someone enjoying it. After the events of the last few hours, she feared it might end its existence as *The Lasagna Destined Never to be Eaten.*

"I'd be glad to." Maddie smiled, sliding the layered pasta onto Sam's empty dish. "It's pretty simple to throw together."

She'd been surprised to see Officer Jessup again since he'd been the one who responded to her call earlier that morning, and she said as much. He explained he was working a double shift since the wife of the officer who'd been scheduled to work had gone into labor three weeks early.

"So what do you think, Bill?" Sam asked before shoveling another forkful into his mouth. He followed it with a big gulp of iced tea that emptied his glass and Maddie rose automatically to refill it. She'd been bustling around the kitchen for the past hour trying to keep her mind off the fact that someone had been in her house and had gone through her things. Beyond creepy in itself, coupled with the message on her laptop screen, she had little success in taming the quivering mess sloshing in her stomach.

"I don't know what to think, frankly. There's no sign of forced entry, and nothing was taken. Is there anyone else who might have a key?"

Sam shook his head and swallowed another bite before replying. "Not that I know of. The lawyer sent Maddie one, I have one, and I gave Frank's to Jeff Hagen this afternoon. It's in the lock-box on the front door, but I already checked, and it doesn't appear to have been tampered with."

"Well, the message on the computer screen seems pretty personal. Anyone else have the password?" Bill asked.

"No password. It never seemed necessary, and I'm not very good at remembering things like that," Maddie confessed. "I'm not very computer savvy, quite honestly. I only use it for email and to keep a database of my paintings. You know…if they're in a gallery, what sold, when, how much…that kind of thing. There isn't anything on there that would be important to anyone else."

Maddie set Sam's glass next to him and started to turn back to the counter to flick on the coffeemaker and get dessert plates for the fruit. Sam's hand shot out, and his fingers closed around her arm. His thumb stroked her wrist in the most distracting way. Her pulse jumped in response. She wondered if he even realized he was doing it.

"Madigan, sit down and eat something," he said quietly.

"I'm not very hungry," she admitted, touched by his concern. They stared into one another's eyes for long minutes until Bill cleared his throat loudly, breaking the spell.

"You're sure there's nothing missing?" Bill asked for the second time. Maddie tore her gaze from Sam's reluctantly.

"Well, I guess there could be. I mean, I have no idea what my father had, so I wouldn't have a clue if something of his was gone, but as nearly as I can tell, nothing of mine seems to have been touched," Maddie replied. "Weren't there some recent break-ins in Greeley? Sam told me about it earlier."

"Oh, and someone broke into her place in the city tonight, too," Sam added.

"You didn't mention that before." Bill's brows drew together in a frown. "Maybe this is connected. Maddie, is there anyone you've had a problem with? Anyone you can think of that might have followed you here?"

She thought about it for a moment then shook her head resolutely. "No, no one."

"Okay, then. I'll file the report when I get back to the station, and I'll arrange to increase the patrols in the neighborhood. Other than that, I'm afraid there isn't much we can do. Keep your doors locked, and give me a call if you notice anything suspicious." Maddie nodded and Bill pushed his chair back, groaning his way to his feet after declining the fruit and coffee.

"I've never known a cop to refuse coffee," Maddie teased. "I bet you'd stay if I had doughnuts instead of apples."

"Now that's downright insulting." Bill laughed. "You shouldn't buy into stereotypes. Besides, I have to go right past the Dippin' Donuts on my way back downtown, and it just so happens my patrol car only knows how to get back to the square by way of their drive-through."

Bill and Sam shook hands at the door, and after thanking Maddie again for dinner, Bill reminded her about the recipe. She promised to write it down and give it to Sam.

"Try not to worry too much, Maddie. Sometimes I feel like I'm a cop in Mayberry. Teenagers fighting over a girl at the church picnic, parking tickets, fender benders, and the occasional domestic dispute are pretty much the highlights of my career. The crime rate here is so low it's almost nonexistent. Not that I'm complaining. Maybe you're right, and this is someone's poor idea of a joke." Bill patted Maddie's arm.

"I hope so." She smiled, but she didn't believe it. Judging by the tight set of Sam's jaw, he didn't either. Maddie watched Bill climb in his patrol car, waved him off, then closed and locked the door. Sam had already gone back into the kitchen, and by the time Maddie returned, he'd cleared the table, put the leftover lasagna in the fridge, and poured them both a cup of coffee.

"Thanks." She collapsed into the chair and pulled the mug toward her. "I should probably see if there's a bigger cup in the house. I have a hunch I'll need all the caffeine I can get tonight. Don't imagine I'll be sleeping much."

"Don't take this the wrong way, but maybe I should stay here tonight. I mean, I'll sleep in Frank's room or on the couch or something," he hurried to add when Maddie's shocked gaze flew to his face. "But I don't think you should be here on your own until the police figure this out."

"I hate this!" Maddie cried. "I shouldn't have to be afraid to sleep in my own house. I hate that someone has the power to make me feel this way. Why would anyone do this, Sam? No one even knows me here anymore."

"I have no idea, but I'm going to talk to Bill again tomorrow. I want him to contact the GPD and see if there are any similarities to the cases there." Sam reached for her hand. She linked her fingers with his. She was glad he was here. She'd been tempted to walk away and not look back earlier when he'd confessed his problem. He owed her nothing, yet he'd told her the truth when he had to know her potential reaction. That should count for something.

"I'd like to think it's just some harmless creep," Maddie said. "But then why take the trouble to go through my things, find my laptop, and leave that message? That seems so…personal." She couldn't suppress the shudder that ran through her. She felt like someone watched her even now, almost as though the walls had eyes. She knew the feeling wasn't going to go away any time soon, and certainly not tonight.

"So, what do you think about me staying?" Sam prompted.

Maddie took a deep breath and considered the man in front of her. There was still an undeniable chemistry between them, and Maddie already felt a little too attached for her own good. She was starting to depend on him, and she'd learned the hard way the only one she could depend on was herself.

"Aren't you worried about what the neighbors will say?" Maddie hedged. "You did warn me this is a small town where everyone knows everyone else's business. I'm only here temporarily, but you have to live with these people. I wouldn't want you to tarnish your reputation on my account."

"I'll take my chances." He grinned.

"Oh, so you're a rebel!" Sam Barstow spending the night might be its own brand of trouble. "Well, even though I *would* feel a little more comfortable with someone in the house, at least for tonight, I'm not sure it's such a great idea for a lot of reasons." Although staring into those amazing blue eyes, at the moment she had trouble remembering exactly what any of those reasons were.

"It's no problem, but it's your call. Let's make sure everything is locked up tight as a drum before I leave then, huh?" He rose to his feet, and Maddie trailed along behind him as he checked every door and window on both floors. He even thought to throw the bolt on the door in the kitchen that led to the basement since there was an outside access.

"There, that should do it." He halted at the front door, dropping a big hand on her shoulder and giving it a gentle squeeze. "Lock the door after me, and I'll see you tomorrow. Call if you need anything, or if you change your mind about staying here alone."

"Thanks, Sam. I do appreciate it." Maddie's eyes searched his face, and she involuntarily reached out a hand to cup his sculpted jaw. She couldn't remember the last time someone had actually worried about her. She'd been fighting her own battles for as long as she could remember, and today it felt almost as though she belonged to a team. She liked feeling less alone for a change.

The pressure of Sam's fingers increased slightly, and Maddie stepped closer. She saw the question in his eyes and didn't hesitate to raise her face to his. His breath feathered along her jaw before he covered her slightly parted lips with his own warm, firm ones. She melted against him, and the kiss deepened and evolved into something so much more than the brief offer of comfort Maddie suspected he'd intended it to be. She hesitated, her fingers curled tightly against his stomach, but then surrendered to the riot of feelings the kiss evoked and allowed her hands to slide up the hard planes of his chest to twine around his neck. His arm circled her waist, and he pulled her more intimately against him. She felt the hard evidence of his desire pressing insistently against her stomach, and she was lost. She'd spent so many years carefully keeping people at a distance. For the first time in a long time, Sam Barstow made her want to let someone in. She wanted this man, and not just because he was trip over your own feet sexy. She wanted the whole package. She always had. She'd forced herself to forget because it hurt too much to remember. Considering her stay here was temporary, letting him back in might not be the best decision she'd ever make, but hell, she'd made worse.

When Sam raised his head at last, Maddie saw the passion clouding his gaze. She felt sure he must see the same in hers. His breathing rasped unevenly, and hers sounded no better.

"See you tomorrow," he panted.

"Okay," she gasped, releasing him reluctantly.

"Lock the door."

"Uh huh." Additional conversation seemed beyond her at the moment.

Sam stepped out into the night, and Maddie closed the door securely behind him. She leaned against it weakly until her legs would hold her. She heard the truck start and crunch out of the drive, and she reached to turn the lock, engaging the deadbolt. She wished she could think of an equally foolproof method to safeguard her heart. She had a sinking feeling she might need one.

Since Sam had already cleared away the remains of their dinner, Maddie simply washed their coffee mugs and rinsed the pot. Then she went into the living room and shut down her laptop, carefully averting her eyes from the scrolling message still dancing across the screen. She tucked the computer under her arm and slowly climbed the stairs, thinking she might take another quick shower. She realized how ridiculous it was that it would be her third today, but the thought of someone going through her things had left her feeling dirty. She paused at the top of the stairs and opened the door to the back bedroom. When they'd gone through it with Jeff earlier in the day, she'd thought it might make a good studio space. She wondered if the town boasted an art supply store, or maybe she'd have better luck finding supplies at the mall Sam had mentioned. She made a mental note to ask him tomorrow. Since it was dark, she couldn't judge the quality of the light that would be there during the day, but she certainly had enough room to work and then some. There were two doors in the room. The first opened to a closet similar in size to the one in her room. The second concealed a dark stairwell leading to the attic. The musty dark chill of the space had always given her the creeps. She heard a faint thump, and then a board squeaked overhead. She froze, then shook her head at her own foolishness. No matter how her father had modernized it, she'd inherited an old house. Old houses settle. Despite her pep talk, she shivered as she clicked off the light and left the room pulling the door firmly closed.

Maddie placed a trembling hand on the doorknob to her father's room, swallowed hard, and pushed it open. She wasn't sure what she'd been expecting, but no bogeymen or memory ghosts jumped out to grab her. It was just a room. She assumed the pile of boxes stacked against one wall contained her father's clothes. Maddie decided she actually did want to go through them herself before donating them in case she found something she wanted to keep. In the corner were piles of books that had always resided in the built-ins on the sides of the fireplace. Propped next to them, a framed painting faced the wall. As Maddie bit her lip and bent to move the books aside, the painting pitched forward and clattered to the floor of its own accord. She gasped, and then gingerly grasped the edge of the frame and turned it around. When the subject was revealed, her heart lurched painfully.

"Well, damn." Maddie propped it back against the wall facing out and stepped back on trembling legs. Sitting down hard on the bed, she took a long, shuddering breath. It was a street scene. It could have been a street in any small town in America. But it wasn't. It was *her* small town, this town, the one in which she'd been born. In the center of the painting a laughing little girl with big, green eyes and curly brown pigtails exited a half opened door, her arm reaching back and clinging tightly to a hand, all that was visible of the unseen man who remained inside the building. In the girl's other hand a blue ice pop melted, running down her chubby fingers. A crinkled paper bag overflowing with licorice whips peeked from the front pocket of her red overalls. Maddie had painted it over eight years ago. It was the first painting she'd ever sold, in the first gallery showing she'd ever had. When she'd asked the gallery owner who bought it, wanting to send a thank you note, she was told the buyer had paid cash and wished to remain anonymous.

"You were there," she whispered brokenly to the empty room. "You were there, and I never even knew. Well, aren't you just full of surprises, Dad?" She wondered if it would have made any difference in how she'd reacted to his attempt at a reconciliation, and honestly didn't know. She did know regret would be a footnote inscribed on her heart for all time.

Maddie released an unsteady breath and rose to her feet. Picking up the painting, she left the room, pulling the door closed with a decisive click. She leaned the painting against the wall and continued down the hall to drop her laptop on the bed in her own room. Then she grabbed the painting again on her way downstairs.

A nail still protruded from the wall over the fireplace where the painting had hung before being removed for the renovations. She hefted it into place and stood back. Every Friday night, the same group of raucous men in sweat-stained shirts gathered for a Friday night poker game in her mother's cramped kitchen. Maddie would rush downstairs as soon as she woke up the next day to crawl among the cold, chrome legs of the kitchen chairs and gather the coins that had fallen from the table to the beer-sticky floor. She smiled faintly to herself at the fuzzy memory of the licorice whips, two-cent ice pops, and shared laughter with her father on the short walks home from Wartella's store every Saturday morning. The store closed long ago, her father died, and she sure as hell wasn't that optimistic, naïve little girl anymore. Still, the scene represented one of her happiest memories. Without ever realizing it before, Maddie understood now she had unconsciously done the painting for her father. And somehow, miraculously it had ended up right where it belonged. Maybe he'd understood the unspoken message contained in the brushstrokes.

"Maybe he did know," she whispered, trying hard to believe it. It made her heart feel slightly less heavy to think about it that way.

Maddie sucked in a breath between her teeth as a cool breeze came from nowhere, smelling of cherry tobacco, and ruffled her hair. She spun to face the empty room as the lights dimmed and flickered. Her gaze darted wildly, but just like when she'd heard the voice, there was nothing to be seen. She was losing her mind. Or maybe she so badly wanted to believe there was still some way to make things right, her mind was playing tricks. Maddie didn't believe in ghosts, at least not the incorporeal kind that hung around after death. The ones inhabiting her mind were another matter altogether. She concentrated on her breathing until her heart resumed a normal rhythm. Yes…it had been an exhausting, stressful few days, and her mind was playing tricks on her. That was all.

Maddie grabbed her cell phone and hurried back up

the stairs to her room. Gathering her robe, boxers, and tank top, she headed for the bathroom. She made quick work of her shower, her ears cocked toward the door for any unusual sound. She hopped out and briskly toweled off, still damp when she belted her robe tightly and went back to her room. She loved the comfortable understated elegance and longed to climb into the bed and snuggle beneath the heavy comforter and pull it over her head like a protective shield. But after the evening she'd had, her nerves wouldn't allow her to sleep upstairs. She and her new best friend, the television, were going to spend the night together once again.

****

Sam checked in at the local convenience store for coffee and a bag of cheddar popcorn in case he wanted a snack later. After topping off his gas tank, he circled back and pulled into an empty parking spot across the street and a few doors down from Maddie's place. She'd considered it a bad idea for him to spend the night for a lot of reasons, and he couldn't honestly disagree. But after that kiss, he had a damn hard time remembering what any of them were. Madigan might not want him to stay, but he damn sure couldn't go home and leave her unprotected with a clear conscience, either. Sam decided he'd compromise by setting up his own little surveillance for the night. After all, once upon a time, he'd been the best. He believed Bill would increase the patrols like he promised, but with a police department the size of Pine Grove's, that pretty much meant a cruiser might pass by the house twice during the night instead of once. Sam harbored no illusions. This wasn't someone's idea of a prank. It was personal. Someone had gotten into and out of that house unobserved, and knew enough about breaking and entering to have done it undetected, leaving only the evidence he wanted to leave.

Sam pushed the truck seat back as far as it would go, but found he still didn't have enough leg room to be anything approaching comfortable. He wished he'd brought the car. A reclining seat would have been a hell of a lot more practical. He popped the lid off the Styrofoam cup and took a long, fortifying swig. He had a hunch he would need all the caffeine he could get to make it through the night. He huddled down into the quilted flannel he'd pulled from behind the seat. The temperature dropped like a stone once the sun went down. He forced his mind away from the thought of how much warmer it would be in Maddie's bed with her hot skin pressed against his. He might tell himself he didn't believe in love anymore, but apparently, his faith in lust was still alive and well. It was going to be a long night.

Chapter Nine

Maddie grabbed the pillows from the bed and stuffed them under her arm. Just because she was sleeping on the couch didn't mean she had to use those hard as a rock throw pillows again. She had just reached the bottom of the stairs when someone rapped sharply on the door. Half hoping it might be Sam refusing to take no for an answer, she clicked the deadbolt, left the chain engaged, and cracked open the door. To her surprise, Bill Jessup had returned.

"Hi, Bill." She smiled, sliding the chain free and opening the door to let him in. "Back for seconds?"

"Don't tempt me, woman." He smiled back, stepping into the hall. "I still can't fasten my belt from earlier. Actually, I'm just getting off duty. Finally. But I found out a couple things I thought you should be aware of."

"Oh?"

"Yeah," he continued, no longer smiling. "I got to thinking about what you told me earlier about the break-ins over in Greeley and decided to check it out. The reports from the GPD were coming through the fax as I left, so I waited to see what they had to offer."

"And?" The trill of Maddie's cell interrupted the conversation. She glanced at the display and hit the accept button. "Excuse me a minute, Bill. Sam?"

"Hi. Just wanted to double check and make sure

you were okay."

"Yeah, I'm fine. Um, Bill stopped by. Says he has some news."

"Okay, hang tight…I can be back there in a sec."

The line went dead and Maddie turned back to Bill.

"That was Sam. He'll be here in a minute if you want to wait and not tell the story twice. C'mon in and have a seat. Can I get you something cold to drink or maybe a cup of coffee?"

"I wouldn't refuse a glass of iced tea if it's not too much trouble." He tossed his hat on the armchair and followed it down with a weary sigh. "I'm gonna give my wife a call and let her know I'm running a little late. She worries."

"I'm sure she does." As Maddie moved toward the kitchen, she heard the sound of someone pulling into the drive. Sam returned in record time. Her heart skipped a beat thinking of the kiss they'd shared earlier. She knew she'd passed the point where she would offer much of an argument if he wanted to take that kiss a little further. And if he suggested staying again? Well, she probably wouldn't offer much of an argument there, either. Letting Sam Barstow back into her life might be a danger to her heart, but she couldn't ignore the feeling he might be the best thing she'd ever had in her life. If she was wrong and doomed to pay for it later, so be it.

She heard the front door open, and her pulse quickened at the rich timbre of his voice as he greeted Bill.

"Iced tea, Sam?" she called.

"I'm good, Maddie, thanks."

Maddie came back into the parlor and set Bill's drink on the table beside him. She sank down on the sofa next to Sam and waited while Bill took a long swig before speaking.

"Well, turns out there *were* a couple break-ins over in Greeley. Nothing taken but women's lingerie. Both women were living alone. I have calls out to all the departments within a twenty mile radius to see if there were any other incidents."

"Any leads on the Greeley cases?" Sam asked curtly.

Bill nodded his head slowly. "Actually, they caught the guys and charged them. The hearing is pending. Turns out it was a couple college kids involved in a pledge week prank. A new twist on the traditional panty raid."

"But?" Maddie prompted, sensing Bill had more to say and it wasn't going to be something she wanted to hear. She unconsciously reached for Sam's hand, and he wrapped her cold fingers in his.

"Well, all things considered, I doubt there's any connection to what happened here tonight. Frankly, Madigan, I'm not so sure you should be staying here alone. We don't know who we're dealing with or what the motive might be. It couldn't hurt to stay at a hotel for the night."

"Maybe so, but the likelihood of you catching this guy tonight is pretty slim, and I can't stay at a hotel indefinitely. Besides, while I admit I'm nervous, I refuse to let someone run me out of my own home. Sam made sure everything is locked up good and tight, and I still have a can of pepper spray in my purse," Maddie announced with more bravado than she felt.

"I understand where you're coming from, but I just don't like the idea of you staying here alone," Bill said.

"Why don't I call my wife? Maybe you could…"

"She's not staying here alone," Sam interjected firmly, jumping to his feet and pulling Maddie to hers. He freed his fingers and threw an arm around her shoulders hauling her against him. Bill glanced from one to the other and lifted a brow over his suddenly twinkling eyes while a slow, devious-looking smile curled his lips.

"I see," he drawled knowingly.

"Get your mind out of the gutter, Bill," Sam muttered. "Maddie is justifiably nervous after what happened, and I'll be sleeping on the couch."

"Naturally." Bill's smile had morphed into a shrewd smirk.

"I did warn you about your reputation," Maddie stage whispered.

"It's not *my* reputation I'm thinking about."

"Well, I won't be here long enough for mine to matter one way or the other," Maddie replied too quickly and wondered why the thought didn't cheer her as much as it had even a day ago.

"Sorry to hear that, Maddie." Bill frowned. "I hope this whole sordid episode isn't the reason. We'll get this creep."

"No, actually I always intended to sell the place and go back to the city. And besides, I have a responsibility to my roommate. She depends on my half of the rent. But if any place could tempt me to stay, I think Pine Grove might be it. It's a great place to live." The truth of the statement surprised her. After years convincing herself she hated Pine Grove, the longer she stayed, the more attached to the house and tempted by the town, she became. Creepy intruder notwithstanding.

The realization surprised her as much as the unexpected grief over her father's death. But even if she wanted to stay, she couldn't simply walk away without giving Chris a chance to find another roommate.

"It *is* a great place to live," Bill confirmed. "Well, I need to get home. It's been one hell of a long day. Keep your eyes and ears open, and give me a call if anything seems strange. Sam, I'll see you at the game. You coming, Maddie?" Bill hauled himself out of the chair and headed for the door.

"Oh! I don't know," she hedged, glancing over at Sam. "I'm not much of a sports girl."

"Yep, we'll be there after she's done at Caroline's. One of the waitresses quit, and Maddie offered to help out until Caroline can find someone to fill in," Sam interjected without hesitation, as though it had been a foregone conclusion.

"Hey, that's nice of you, Maddie. Caroline's a peach, but she works too damn hard, and she's not as young as she used to be. Okay, then...see you both tomorrow. Maddie, don't forget that recipe, huh?"

"Actually, I already wrote it down. Let me grab it for you before you go," Maddie offered with a smile and started into the kitchen as Bill turned to Sam with a slight frown. It was a small house, and as she retrieved the recipe from the counter, Maddie could still hear every word. Neither man seemed to notice when she paused on her way back to observe the entire exchange from the doorway.

Bill Jessup scrubbed a hand over his face. "Sam, I know you better than most people, but after what happened tonight, someone who didn't know you so well might not assume you were parked down the street watching the house because you're a good guy. Let's face it, with your background and expertise, breaking and entering is a piece of cake."

Maddie gasped from the doorway. Her eyes flew to Sam's face, which had begun to darken as a flush crept up his neck. He'd been parked down the street watching the house? No wonder he'd been able to get here so quickly when Bill showed up.

"Is that why you stopped by, Bill, to warn Maddie I might be some closet perv?"

He kept his tone light, but Maddie easily detected the underlying anger. Apparently, Bill Jessup detected it too, because he stepped right up to Sam until they were almost nose-to-nose.

"I stopped by because I was worried about Madigan staying here alone. The department doesn't have the manpower to have someone watching the house twenty-four-seven. Obviously, you know that, as well as I do, since you were hunkered down out there like the Undercover Avenger."

Madigan watched anxiously as the two men stared one another down. Finally, Sam's shoulders visibly relaxed, and Bill grinned.

"Hell, Sam if I knew you were watching the place, I wouldn't have even bothered to stop by. That alone should tell you something. I'm just telling you to watch your ass. Not everyone would see it that way."

"Yeah, well." Sam's eyes flicked to Maddie. She steeled her features into a calm expression.

"Anyway, since you're staying, I can go home and get a good night's sleep. Damn, I'm beat." Bill indulged in a jaw-cracking yawn as Maddie moved into the room to hand him the recipe. He glanced at it with a smile then tucked it in the pocket of his shirt. "Thanks. G'night, Maddie."

"Goodnight, Bill and thanks for stopping by to check on me." Bill pulled the door open and Madigan followed to close it behind him and engage the lock.

"Look," Maddie began awkwardly turning to Sam. "I appreciate you offering to stay tonight, I really do. I admit I'm a little shaky, but you don't have to put yourself out like this."

Sam laughed without humor. "I don't remember complaining, but given what I told you earlier, combined with what you just heard, I can understand if you'd feel safer with me outside the house rather than inside."

"Don't be ridiculous," Maddie snapped. "You're hardly a stranger and besides, you have a key remember? If I thought for a New York minute you had anything to do with this, I'd be showing you the other side of the door and asking for it back, don't you think?"

Sam dug in his pocket and pulled out a heavy ring of keys. He worked one free and held it out to her. "Here. Take it."

Maddie crossed her arms over her chest. "I don't want it."

"You should. You may have known me once, but you don't know anything about who I am now."

"Maybe, but I could say the same. Some things never change, and I think I still know you well enough to be certain you had nothing to do with this. Let's face it Sam, if you wanted to get your hands on me, we're both aware you wouldn't need to break in to do it."

The faint hiss of a swiftly indrawn breath was the

only indication he hadn't expected such blunt honesty. His piercing blue eyes never left her face as he blindly worked the key back onto the ring and dropped the whole thing back in his pocket.

"Why did you leave, Madigan?" He stepped closer.

"What does it matter now?" She took a step in his direction.

"It matters." Another step and Maddie's heart pounded uncomfortably.

"It's ancient history." Her feet seemed to move of their own accord.

"You rearranged the kitchen."

"So?" Maddie raised her brows in confusion at the sudden change in topic.

"You hung your painting over the fireplace."

"What does that have to do with anything?"

"You're nesting."

"I'm what?"

"Nesting, making this your home."

"I am?"

"Aren't you?"

"No, of course not. If I'm going to be here for a while, I might as well be comfortable. It's not the same thing at all."

"If you say so."

"I say so," she replied firmly, but even to her own ears, her voice lacked conviction.

One more step and he stood so close she could feel the heat radiating from his body through the flimsy barrier of her robe. His bright blue eyes had darkened to the deep indigo of a tempestuous sky on the verge of a wild storm, and her heartbeat thrummed in response to the fire blazing there. Breath rushed painfully into her lungs as smoldering heat curled low in her stomach, then spread outward leaving her trembling. Pressing her thighs together, she fought the urge to squirm. She stared at the face she'd never truly forgotten. It was older, lined with history she hadn't been a part of. But, she saw the same chiseled jaw, the high cheekbones, and that damn dimple that had always made her heart flip-flop in her chest every time he flashed it in her direction. She remembered brushing her lips along the long, smooth column of his throat, tasting the salty sheen of his sweat, pressing her lips to that delicious spot where it joined his shoulder. She swallowed hard and a shiver rolled over her skin.

"Maybe some things never do change," he whispered hoarsely. "We always did affect each other like a match to kindling."

"Yeah, I guess we did," she breathed raggedly. She thought of the way he'd held her when she'd been overcome by the sight of the backyard. The way he'd covered her ass about her absence at Frank's funeral. This was crazy. It could never go anywhere. They weren't two horny teenagers anymore. But they were both consenting adults. She wanted him and he wanted her, like always. And for a little while, she needed to know someone did. Just for tonight. Maybe tomorrow could take care of itself.

His reached to pull her close and lowered his head to capture her mouth. Maddie leaned into him with a sigh. His hands slid inside her robe, and while one splayed across the small of her back, the other cupped her buttocks through the thin barrier of her boxers and pulled her more intimately against him. He rocked his hips, and desire consumed her right down to her fingertips as the hard evidence of his desire ground insistently against the juncture of her thighs. Bad idea or not, she wanted this. She wanted him.

His mouth slanted over hers, his tongue probing, stroking, and tangling frantically with hers, again and again, as they stumbled across the room in the general direction of the stairs. They never made it. Somehow, her robe disappeared and clothing lay strewn across the floor. The back of her knees hit the sofa and her legs buckled. He followed her down, and his hands were everywhere at once. Her shower fantasies hadn't even come close to the addictive sensation of his hands stroking her heated flesh. Maddie felt as though she might go up in flames as his calloused fingers cupped her breast, and he dragged a heavy thumb across a straining nipple.

"So damned soft," he murmured against her neck.

Her fingers fumbled with the zipper on his jeans. And his groan seemed to come from somewhere deep in his soul when she finally succeeded in freeing his straining erection and wrapped her fingers around him. He groaned again as he reached to pry her fingers away, lifted them to his lips, and then climbed to his feet to shove his jeans and boxers down and kick them off before covering her body with his big, warm one again. He captured her mouth for a gentle kiss, then nipped lightly at her lower lip before drawing back to lean his forehead against hers.

"God, you're beautiful."

"You don't have to suck up, you know. You've already got me pretty much where you want me."

"I don't do sucking up. You do own a mirror, right?"

"Of course, but while I don't see myself in the ugly crone category, I've never thought of myself as beautiful, either. I'm talented, but not gifted, intelligent, but not genius, someone who tries to do the right thing, but falls far short more often than not. Overall? Average. And that's okay by me. I'm quite comfortable in my mediocrity."

"You've never been mediocre, Madigan Moran. And as for having you where I want you, the bed would be a helluva lot more comfortable than this sofa."

"True. But it sure beats a cramped back seat."

"Good point." Sam dipped his head to feather his lips along the line of her jaw before burying his face in her neck and nipping gently at the sensitive spot where it met her shoulder. Her weak spot, the one he'd always resorted to when he wanted to drive her crazy. As his lips and tongue worked their way up the side of her throat, she realized it still did. He still did.

Maddie squirmed restlessly beneath him, reveling in the friction of his skin against hers. As his fingers fondled and teased, relearning every inch of her, through half closed lids her gaze traced every line, every flexed muscle of the man he'd become. A man of hard planes and sharp angles and work roughened hands. Hands that were surprisingly gentle as he slipped one between their bodies, and his long, clever fingers stroked her with an expertise she feared might drive her mad. She couldn't speak, couldn't think. Time ceased to exist. His hot breath coming in short, ragged bursts against the side of her neck drove her to the brink. Anticipation tightened her gut, adding to the delicious sensations gathering at her core. She arched against him with a moan, seeking release.

Hardly able to wait another second, Maddie worked her hand between their slick bodies and curled her fingers around him, firmly stroking the hot, silken flesh from root to tip. Sam responded with a guttural moan that clawed its way out of his chest and past his lips. While one hand continued to tease her slick folds, the other groped beside the couch for his discarded jeans, until he triumphantly displayed a foil packet, and tore it open with his teeth. Sam swore under his breath as he fumbled with the package. Maddie tugged it from his shaking fingers, pulled the condom free, and slowly rolled the sheath down the impressive length of his shaft after tossing the foil package over her head.

"Executive protection?" Maddie giggled, her mind still cloudy with passion.

"Nothing but the best for you, kid."

He positioned himself between her thighs, rested on top of her, and supported his weight with his forearms. Dipping his head to her breast, he rolled a hard nipple between his lips, nipping lightly and easing the sting with his tongue. Suddenly he lifted his head, his expression an equal mix of rampant desire and haunting uncertainty, and his body stilled.

"What's wrong?" she gasped.

"Why did you leave?" he whispered tightly. Beads of perspiration dotted his forehead.

"*Now*? You're asking me that *now*? Is it so important at this precise moment?"

"I just…this isn't…I don't want you to have any regrets about this."

The unspoken subtext was clear. He wasn't planning to pick up where they'd left off. He was doing his part to quench a mutual fire. They weren't making love. They were having sex. Maddie ignored the curious little pang in the region of her heart and pushed away the doubt. She was a big girl, and her eyes were wide open.

"The only thing I'm going to regret is if you can't finish what you started."

"You're sure?"

"Well, if you don't think you're up for it..."

"Lady, you have no idea," he growled. He lowered his head with slow deliberation and captured her lips. The kiss was slow, teasing, and exquisitely gentle. Maddie pushed aside any lingering doubts as all control slipped away, and she gave in to the sensations reverberating through her body. Her heart clenched, and her stomach muscles tightened in anticipation of the approaching storm. They'd always been good together, but they'd been two, fumbling teens. Maturity and experience on both sides added a whole new dimension and promised to take her to a place she'd never been.

"Sam?" She tore her mouth free and gasped against his lips. "Now."

She didn't have to ask twice. Already saturated with her arousal, as he positioned a hand on either side of her head and speared into her in one deep thrust, her body opened for him like butter to a hot knife. Maddie moaned long and low as he filled the emptiness within her, an emptiness that had nothing to do with physical need and everything to do with the absence of this particular man in her life for so long. Even before her muscles relaxed enough to comfortably accommodate him, he hammered hard and deep, quickening his pace as her thighs quivered and her body tightened around him. She bit into her lower lip and dug her fingers into his hard, sweat slicked shoulders where they bunched tensely under her hands. Sam's gaze glued to her face. He clenched his jaw and adjusted his angle, and her body writhed beneath him as he drove deeper and faster with an urgency bordering on desperation.

He bucked against her, the penetration deeper and fuller with every thrust. Maddie clenched her teeth together and gripped his shoulders even tighter as her body ached and pulsed. He slammed into her over and over, and she rose to meet him every time, allowing his urgent rhythm to drive her higher, hotter, burning like an uncontrolled wildfire toward something she wasn't sure she could survive. Just as she went over the edge, her body tightening around him and every nerve in her body exploding, he thrust into her with a hoarse shout and enough force to lift her body from the sofa before collapsing on top of her with a moan.

"My God…that was…unexpected." He panted against her neck as he rolled slightly to the side to relieve her of his weight while they floated slowly back to earth. A shudder went through him. When he raised his head, his eyes burned with some intense emotion she couldn't read. He stroked her damp curls away from her forehead and then drew a finger along her cheek to trace her lips. The unconsciously tender gesture made Maddie's eyes fill reflexively. She blinked the moisture away before he could see. He didn't mean anything by it. He'd as much as told her so, right? She shook her head slightly and turned her face away. It was just sex, nothing more.

"Hey, you okay?" he asked softly.

"Unexpected? Dammit, Sam. I didn't expect any of this."

"Any of what?"

"The grief, the memories, the feeling of belonging…you."

She felt him tense against her.

"Sorry. Didn't mean to go all philosophical." She turned back and pasted on a smile. "Just catching my breath. That was…wow."

"Definitely wow." He flashed the dimple. He pushed up and levered his body away from hers, holding the condom in place with his thumb and forefinger. Cool air replaced the heat of his body, and Maddie shivered, feeling the loss. Sam tugged the throw from the back of the sofa and tucked it around her.

"Hang on, I'll be right back. Let me take care of this."

Maddie huddled under the blanket admiring the view as Sam unselfconsciously strode into the kitchen and on through to the bathroom. He'd been honest, and he'd been clear. So why this tightness in her throat, this ache in her chest? Why this feeling they'd just shared something profound? Her eyes stung again. Despite her best intentions, apparently she still hadn't mastered the fine art of casual sex.

She threw her legs over the side of the couch and sat up when she heard the bathroom door open, heralding Sam's return. He tugged the blanket free and dropped down beside her, pulling her into his lap, and settling the blanket over both of them before leaning back in a semireclining position. She stiffened slightly and shot to her feet. She located her robe under the coffee table, and dragged it on before sitting back down next to him rather than on top of him.

"What?" His brows drew together in confusion.

"Nothing, it's just…" Once the mind-melting passion had been temporarily sated, she felt a little self-conscious. "I don't usually do this."

"Have sex?" he grinned.

No, have sex with someone she would always love and couldn't have.

"Are you hungry?" she asked, ignoring his question. She decided she could keep it light, too, or at least die in the attempt. "Hey, I still have those rice cakes."

"Is that your go-to postcoital snack offering?" He laughed.

"Well, you've already had my famous lasagna." She forced herself to grin in return. "I'm not sure we know one another well enough anymore to warrant breaking out my chocolate stash."

"Maybe we need to remedy that," he whispered as though the idea surprised him. He reached for her chin and tilted her face to his, capturing her lips once more.

"So, tell me about your painting." Sam pulled back and settled her under his shoulder.

"Hmm…well, I paint pictures. Sometimes people buy them. Sometimes they don't. End of story." She shrugged.

"I'm sure there's a little more to it than that," he chuckled. "I mean, you were always good, even in high school, but I understand you've been pretty successful. I guess running away to art school paid off, huh?"

"Yeah, I guess," she whispered. It had paid off in one sense and cost her everything in another. "What about you? Do you miss security work?"

"Sometimes. I miss the challenge, the analytic

nature of it, the teamwork. I was good, some said one of the best. But man, I guess it's true the bigger you are, the harder you fall. When I failed? It was epic," Sam responded quietly, appearing lost in thought.

"You want to talk about it?" Maddie asked softly.

"It happened a long time ago." Sam shifted uncomfortably. "Talking about it won't change anything."

"That's perhaps the most unquestionably true statement I've ever heard," she observed quietly. "But, sometimes sharing something makes it feel like less of a burden."

"Sometimes." He sighed, giving her a squeeze. "But not in this case...not when my own arrogance resulted in the death of a child. I was so focused on protecting the scumbag witness for the prosecution, I missed what should have been obvious. They went after the piece of shit by way of his son. Sometimes a kindergarten teacher isn't simply a kindergarten teacher."

The pain and regret were etched on Sam's face. Maddie had no idea how to comfort him, so she did the only thing she could think of. She stretched up and softly kissed his cheek. His smile was fleeting, but he squeezed her against his side again.

"And it cost you your career?" she asked.

"What? Oh, hell no. The investigation showed I wasn't at fault. The powers that be were quite happy to send me along to another assignment."

"But you disagreed with their findings?"

"Something like that. Anyway, after I got out of the hospital I wanted to forget. My father, on the other hand, was more than happy to remind me. Every friggin' chance he got. I guess he saw it as his golden opportunity to bring me back into line with his plans for my life. He never managed to accept I had plans of my own. I saw that kid's face in my head every minute of every day. Between that and the fear my father might have been right about me all along, I started drinking. Heavily. Amnesia and oblivion. The free prize in the bottom of every bottle of tequila." Sam's chuckle held no humor.

"But a temporary one," Maddie whispered.

"Yep." He drew in a deep breath and let it out slowly. "And one that creates a whole set of its own problems. Luckily for me, I never actually hit rock bottom, but I was well on my way. Your father saw the direction I was headed and made it his mission in life to badger the hell out of me until I saw it, too."

"He finally came to grips with his problem and his mistakes, didn't he? I should've given him a chance." Maddie sighed in a sad voice.

"Shoulda, woulda, coulda." Sam nudged her chin up and captured her gaze. "Everyone's got a few of those kicking around. Can't change it. Can only move forward and try to do better."

"And what about your father? When did he finally accept that you have your own plans for your life?"

"He didn't. My father will never accept any point of view that doesn't precisely mirror his. The man will never change. Any acceptance had to come on my part. I've finally accepted I can't change him, and I can't control him, so I work on controlling my reaction to him instead."

"Good call, I guess. Can't be easy for you, though."

"Nothing about Edward Barstow is easy. Never has been."

Maddie considered that for a moment. He certainly hadn't been easy on the few occasions she'd been in his company. In fact, he'd intimidated the living hell out of her, especially that last time.

"No, he never has been," she agreed at last.

"Hey," he said softly, tipping her face back to his. "I'm not my father or anyone remotely like him. I'm the same guy I was five minutes ago, okay?"

"Okay." She really liked the guy he was five minutes ago. Maybe even more than she'd liked the guy she knew ten years ago. Okay, maybe more than liked. Because even though she'd left without a word, even though she seemed to make the wrong decision at every turn, even when by rights he should have turned his back on her, he hadn't. He was here. Maddie knew she was in deep trouble when his lips met hers and this time she actually heard bells ring. Then she realized the sound came from the kitchen counter where she'd left her phone.

"Ignore it," he muttered against her lips.

"I can't." She pulled away reluctantly. "It might be Chris calling back about the locksmith."

"So she'll leave a message, and you can check it later." Sam ran his tongue down the side of her neck, and Maddie tilted her head to give him better access. The feel of Sam's hot mouth against her skin, and the pleasure of his hands stroking her body made Chris, the break-in at the apartment, regrets, and everything else seem far away. He was right, she thought, as the embers of passion flared to life again. Chris could leave a message.

Chapter Ten

"So when were you planning to tell me you were already involved with someone, Madigan?"

Sam scraped the scrambled eggs he'd made into the trash wondering why he'd thought making her breakfast was a good idea. He'd wakened from the best sleep he'd had in years, reluctant to untangle himself from Maddie's soft, warm limbs. He wondered if some alien entity had taken the place of what used to pass for his common sense. He never stayed the night with a woman anymore, and though technically he'd planned to do exactly that last night, he hadn't planned to spend it in her bed. And then he'd had the bright idea to cook them both a big breakfast. It was so domestic, so intimate. Of course, once Maddie came downstairs and checked her phone messages, neither of them had much of an appetite.

Sam couldn't understand the tight ache in his chest. He was a one-night stand kind of guy. He didn't plan a future anymore. He didn't want a relationship. At least he hadn't thought he did. And Maddie had been the one to walk away from him before, so clearly she didn't want one either. Of course, the fact she was apparently already smack dab in the middle of one might explain the reluctance on her part. It shouldn't matter to him one way or the other if she was seeing someone. It gave him the perfect out. And that's what he wanted, right?

That's how he rolled.

"At the risk of being redundant, which was probably moot after the fifth time I said it, I'm not involved with anyone," Maddie replied tersely. "Ian and I are beyond over, and I have no idea what he's doing here or what he wants." Maddie had quickly changed into a T-shirt and jeans after listening to Ian's message. Sam had gotten dressed earlier while she slept.

Maddie dragged a brush through her tangled hair. Glaring at her, Sam dropped the pan into the sink and walked over to lean against the doorjamb of the downstairs bathroom.

"A guy flies hundreds of miles to see you when you've been gone barely forty-eight hours? Seems pretty much like involvement to me."

"Not from where I'm standing. He's a snake, pure and simple, and if he took the time to come down here, he's got an ulterior motive. Bet on it."

Sam levered himself away from the door frame and strode toward the front door. He heard the dull thump as Maddie dropped the brush and hurried along after him.

"Where are you going?"

"Hey, far be it from me to throw a wet blanket on your happy reunion." His jaw clenched so tightly it ached. He vaguely realized he might be in danger of breaking a tooth. He reached for the knob, and she inserted herself between him and the door, laying a restraining hand on his chest.

"Don't go."

"Why? Are you into threesomes?"

Maddie flinched as though she'd been struck.

"That was uncalled for and unfair. I told you, Ian and I are over. A fact I'm sure his wife appreciates. Not that I knew he had one, and he became history the minute I found out. Frankly, I've been ignoring his calls. I didn't tell him where I was, and I have no idea why he's suddenly decided to arrive here uninvited. I don't understand why you're so angry, anyway. You made it perfectly clear last night it was just about sex, and you weren't interested in a relationship, right?"

Sam silently acknowledged the remark *had* been uncalled for, but he wasn't in any mood to apologize. And yeah, he thought he had no interest in a relationship and he'd probably insinuated exactly that, but what in the hell made her think last night was about nothing but the sex? In any event, she should have leveled with him. He'd leveled with her even when he knew the truth might drive her away. He'd let her, of all people, in his head in a way he seldom did with anyone these days.

"You should have told me."

"I had nothing to tell!" Maddie shouted, throwing her hands up in the universal gesture of frustration. "Have I asked you for an accounting of every woman you've ever dated or slept with in the last ten years? You're being a complete ass!"

Sam put his hands on her shoulders and gently moved her away from the door. "Just one of my many talents, I guess."

Sam reached for the knob. It felt oddly cold, and he tugged hard on the door. It didn't budge. Maddie reached out and laid a hand on his arm, and with a growl of frustration and a final yank, he ripped the door open and stepped out onto the porch as a car pulled into the drive. Sam didn't wait for an introduction or, in any way, acknowledge the man getting out of the car. He simply climbed into his truck and drove off. He'd been so careful all these years never to put himself in a position where a woman could make a fool of him again. Turned out his judgment where women were concerned hadn't improved with age. Especially when the woman was Madigan Moran. That must be the reason his gut was tied in knots. He was angry at himself for letting his guard down. Yeah, that was it. Right.

****

"Wow," sighed Maddie wearily. "What a rush!" She folded her apron carefully and stowed it under the counter. It was after two, and she and Caroline had been running around like headless chickens for the past three hours. The crowd had finally thinned out, and Caroline told Maddie to grab a bite to eat and call it a day. Maddie sank onto a stool at the lunch counter and dropped her head onto her folded arms. She was so tired her hair ached. After listening to what Ian had come to say and then throwing his sleazy ass out of her house, she'd hopped in the shower, changed into clean clothes, and waited to see if Sam would realize what a jerk he'd been and come back to drive her to Caroline's as they'd planned. Her heart sank, but she wasn't exactly surprised, when he didn't appear. Apparently, she would be walking. Yeah, well, what had she expected? That whole feeling like a part of a team thing was nothing but her overwrought nerves and a long forgotten dream. A temporary brain cramp. Could happen to anyone.

Before starting her trek to the diner, she'd

transferred the money into Chris' account to cover the cost of the locksmith in response to the text her roommate had sent. Then she made a quick stop next door at Hannah's, grateful she didn't actually have to get up close and personal with Mr. Jinx who simply watched her suspiciously from the back of the sofa as she filled his bowl and gave him fresh water. Allergies were the excuse she planned to use if anyone inquired about her red, swollen eyes, but she actually had no desire to suffer with the real thing.

She jumped when Caroline plunked the plate in front of her, appalled to realize she actually must have dozed off.

"Sorry." She offered the older woman a shame-faced grin.

"Wanna talk about it?" Caroline asked, swiping a rag along the length of the counter before tossing it in the sink and pulling over a stool next to Maddie.

"Nothing to talk about," Maddie lied, taking a big gulp of the milkshake without thinking. She closed her eyes and glued her tongue against the roof of her mouth, counting to ten against the instant brain freeze.

"No? Okay then. I just thought the big, red eyes, the obvious lack of sleep, the fact that you walked here today, coupled with the conspicuous absence of Sam Barstow who eats here nearly every day all might be related. My mistake." Caroline shrugged her meaty shoulders, which sent her earrings into a frenetic dance, and started to heave herself off the stool.

"Sam Barstow is an ass," Maddie mumbled miserably over a hefty bite of the chicken salad sandwich.

"Most men are, honey." Caroline chuckled and

settled back onto the vinyl seat. "It's an inherent abnormality located in some obscure gene on the Y chromosome. What did the big ass do?"

"Someone showed up unexpectedly. Sam jumped to conclusions, then refused to listen to reason."

"This someone a man by any chance?"

Maddie swallowed her food. She nodded shortly, rolling her eyes in the process. She knew Caroline's chicken salad was probably delicious, but today everything tasted like sawdust.

"It seems to me a man doesn't overreact like that unless he's more than a little interested in the woman in question." Caroline narrowed her eyes in Maddie's direction.

"Yeah, well if Sam Barstow is more than a little interested, he has a piss poor way of showing it," Maddie grumbled. "Anyway, it doesn't matter. I'll be gone in a few weeks, and I'll manage fine on my own. I always have."

"I'm sure you will, doll." Caroline patted Maddie's arm. "It's a shame, is all. I thought Sam had gotten past all that," she added almost as an afterthought.

"All what?" Maddie asked, trying and failing to hide her interest. She temporarily forgot about the sandwich and the milkshake. She also conveniently forgot she didn't generally entertain gossip, having been the subject of enough of it as a kid to understand how much it could hurt.

"Did you know Sam used to be married?" At Maddie's nod the other woman continued. "Did he also tell you his wife ran off with another man?"

"No, he neglected to mention that," Maddie replied. Well, that would certainly explain his

140

overreaction. "Did that contribute to the drinking?"

"Nah, he'd gotten his act together before that. Still, knocked him pretty low for a while. Frank stepped in to make sure he didn't pick up a bottle again. The booze cost your father everything. He didn't want to see the same thing happen to Sam."

"You knew? About my father, I mean."

"Of course I knew." Caroline patted Maddie's arm again with a laugh. "Owning the only diner in a one horse town is kind of like being a priest…or a bartender. People tend to confide in you."

"Then why did you play along with that cockamamie story about my missing the funeral because I was out of the country? If my father confided in you, you had to know we hadn't reconciled when he died."

"Because Sam wasn't aware I knew, and he was trying to do something noble by covering your ass out of respect for your father even though he expected to dislike you on sight." Caroline grinned, her overdone lipstick turning it into a Joker-like leer. "Apparently he's changed his mind."

"Yeah, well don't be too sure about that. Guess I can't blame him for his lack of trust. Although there wasn't another man involved, I left him, too. And without a word. I didn't think I had a choice at the time, but now I'm not so sure."

"Did you love him?"

"Of course, I loved him. But Edward Barstow made it very clear there was no room for someone like me in Sam's future. And then, there was my father."

"Your father didn't approve, either?"

Maddie smiled sadly. "No, my father loved Sam.

But there'd been an accident. Dad was drunk at the time. When wasn't he drunk, back then? There was a lawsuit pending and a good chance we'd lose everything, and he'd go to jail. Edward promised he could make it all go away if I agreed to stay away from Sam. No matter what issues I had with my dad, I didn't want him locked away. And I couldn't bear the idea of costing Sam his future. But I also didn't see how I could stay here and eventually watch him move on with someone else. Then I got a letter awarding me a scholarship I didn't even remember applying for, and it seemed like fate."

"Fate?" Caroline grumbled quietly pressing her lips together in a thin line. "Methinks maybe fate had a co-conspirator in the person of Edward Barstow."

"You know, that never even occurred to me at the time," Maddie sighed. "But in retrospect, it makes a lot of sense. Leaving Pine Grove, my father, Sam…had to be the hardest thing I've ever done. I thought it might kill me at first, but in a weird way, maybe it saved me, too."

"Saved you?"

"I started attending ACOA meetings. They showed me I'd stepped right into my mother's shoes, become an enabler, helped me understand I wasn't responsible for my father, couldn't fix him. He had to fix himself. Told me I wasn't wrong to want a life that wasn't spent walking on eggshells and nursing a knot in my gut waiting to see if he'd make it home in one piece, or God forbid, injure or kill someone else in the process."

"ACOA?"

"Adult Children of Alcoholics."

"Ah." Caroline nodded. "Well, they were right.

Frank had to fix himself. And he did, but it's understandable that you'd be afraid to trust in it."

"Anyway, whether I made the right or wrong decision back then, it's all water under the bridge, right?"

"Rivers only flow in one direction," Caroline agreed. "And you need to believe your father was proud of what you accomplished and you should be, too. You're a talented artist, and you've got this fellow who traveled all this way to see you, and—"

"Oh, for the love of God! There is nothing between Ian and me," Maddie groaned in frustration pushing the empty plate away and dropping her head back onto her arms. "If Sam had bothered to stick around for two minutes, he would have known that when I threw the slimeball out."

"You threw him out?" Caroline asked in an odd tone.

"Of course I did." Maddie sighed without picking up her head. "Ian owns an art gallery. Maybe I should have known better, but I guess I was dumb enough, or maybe desperate enough, to be flattered when he showed an interest in me, and my work. Last week, a wife I didn't even know he had knocked on my door. I guess she thought he was worth fighting for, but I sure as hell didn't."

"So what's he doing here?"

Maddie's laugh held no humor. "That's the biggest joke of all. He wasn't even interested in *me*. He came here to try to get my *paintings* back."

"Then he's a fool. Don't you agree, Sam?"

Madigan smiled sleepily into the dark cocoon of her folded arms at Caroline's immediate defense of her, then her eyes flew open, and she snapped her head up so quickly she winced in pain. She rubbed the back of her neck and glanced around furtively, but Caroline had quietly disappeared into the kitchen. Maddie was the only one in the diner except for...

"Sam. How long have you been standing there?"

"Couple minutes. Long enough to realize I acted like an idiot earlier. Although I'd actually come to that conclusion on my own."

Maddie slid from the stool and navigated a wide berth around Sam as she moved behind the counter and rinsed her plate and utensils in the sink, then set them in the nearest dish bin. Keeping the counter between them as a barrier, she found Sam's eyes glued to her.

"Well, if you're waiting for an argument from me, you won't get one. What are you even doing here?"

"I figured I'd grab some lunch."

Maddie didn't answer. She snatched the aluminum tumbler containing the remains of her milkshake from the counter, tipped it to her mouth, and drained what remained in the bottom. Then she rinsed it and added it to the pile in the gray plastic bin. She schooled her expression into one as frosty as the half-melted drink.

"I, uh, didn't expect you'd be here." Sam tried again.

"Really? Well, that's odd considering you were sitting right there when Caroline and I made the arrangements."

"What I mean is, after this morning I thought..." He began in a tight voice.

"You thought what, Sam? Never mind, I can easily imagine what you thought. But you thought wrong."

She was angry and tired and close to dissolving

into tears from the combination. She would damn sure not give in to it and let Sam Barstow think she was crying over him. Because she definitely wasn't. The Sam Barstow she thought she knew had left the building in the blink of an eye, or rather, the jangle of a cell phone. The guy who remained in his place was apparently too busy judging her. Then again, he was here now, right? So maybe after he'd had a little time to think it over he realized she was worth it? Nah, he said it himself, he hadn't expected her to be here. He was probably just hungry.

"Well, as long as I'm here anyway, I guess you could use a ride home."

"Actually, I could have used a ride this morning. No biggie. I've got my second wind and the walk will do me good. Thanks, anyway." She grabbed a rag from the sink and scrubbed at the already pristine countertop with far more force than was strictly necessary considering Caroline had already wiped it down less than ten minutes ago.

She knew he knew she was lying. When she'd made the mistake of glancing in the mirror earlier, her eyes were more red than green, and her face wore an unbecoming shade of pale unsuitable for a person this side of the grave. Anyone with eyes could see how her hands trembled with every purposeful movement. She wasn't sure she had the energy to make it across the diner to the front door let alone make the long walk back to her house, but she would crawl every inch of the way on her hands and knees before she would give him the satisfaction of admitting it.

"Look, Madigan, an idiot can see you're exhausted. I jumped to conclusions. Obviously, I made a mistake."

"Well, if it makes you feel any better, you weren't the only one."

"That pride of yours isn't going to keep you on your feet much longer. Be reasonable. Let me give you a lift," Sam persisted in a frustrated tone.

"I'm sorry, did you just tell me to be reasonable? Oh, because you'd know all about that, right?" Madigan never raised her voice, but she had no doubt all her hurt and anger came across loud and clear. She was simply too tired to make an effort to hide it. With a final, angry swipe, she wadded up the wet rag, feeling a certain kinship with the limp cloth, and tossed it into the sink where it landed with a sad, wet plop. Her throat ached as she turned and stalked away to the other end of the counter to grab her purse.

"You're being childish. I jumped to conclusions, I admit that," Sam responded quietly. "You're tired. Stay angry if you want, but at least let me take you home. I promised your father I'd watch out for you."

"Well, my father is dead, Sam, and I'm a big girl. I can take care of myself and have been doing exactly that for a very long time, so consider yourself absolved of the unwanted responsibility. See you tomorrow, Caroline," she called out in the direction of the kitchen, assuming that was where her new friend had escaped to when Sam came in.

Sam was right. She *was* tired. Tired of trying to be good enough—good enough daughter, good enough friend, good enough artist, good enough lover. No matter how hard she tried, she always managed to fall short. Well, she was done. This emotional rollercoaster was completely out of character for her, and frankly, she was beginning to get on her own nerves. From now on, she would only worry about being good enough for herself. Maddie navigated around the sink and nearly ran into Sam when he moved to block the only exit from behind the counter.

"What were you and Caroline talking about when I first came in? I thought I heard her mention my father."

"Enjoy your lunch, Sam."

She stepped around him and walked out the front door without a backward glance.

****

Sam watched her go wishing he had the flexibility to kick himself in the ass. He'd overheard enough of Maddie and Caroline's conversation to confirm he'd been a complete jerk. Furthermore, he had no doubt Caroline had intended he should be made aware of exactly that very thing. Though she'd known him for years, and Maddie for only a few days, she'd easily seen all the good things he remembered about Maddie. Things he'd tried so hard to forget, things he'd been trying so hard to ignore. Caroline had no problem letting him know she thought he was the bad guy. Hell, he didn't need anyone to point it out, he'd realized it all by himself. Well, as soon as he managed to calm his ass down and see the situation objectively, anyway. Madigan had been willing to give him the benefit of the doubt, but he'd chosen his pride over extending her the same courtesy. Maybe he hadn't meant to get involved, but he sure as hell hadn't intended to hurt her, either. This is why he should have stayed away. This, and the dull ache in his chest that told him taking Madigan Moran to bed hadn't worked out the way he expected it would. It hadn't gotten her out of his system at all. It only planted her more firmly in his heart, right where he suspected she'd always been. It shouldn't hurt so much to lose what you didn't even realize you wanted.

Chapter Eleven

Any hopes Maddie had for a little shut-eye were dashed quickly as a big, brown delivery truck pulled into the curb in front of the house just as she dragged her weary butt up the front walk. A kid who didn't even appear old enough to drive, dressed in a brown uniform that matched the truck, climbed down from the driver's seat and hailed her from the street. Apparently, her paintings had arrived. The young man approached with a jaunty swagger.

"Miss Moran?"

"Yes," Maddie sighed wearily.

"Delivery for you." He smiled and handed her a clipboard.

Maddie scribbled her name on the dotted line, and he hustled back to the truck. Maddie unlocked the door and held it open while he brought the crate inside. She'd forgotten how many pieces had been on consignment at Ian's gallery and realized she would never be able to get the huge shipping container upstairs to the room she was considering for a studio. Not by herself. Neither could she leave it in the middle of the living room. There was barely enough space to walk when the driver brought it in. Fortunately, for an extra twenty bucks, the young man agreed to haul it upstairs.

The crate was large and awkward, and he started

up the stairs backwards, dragging the crate by the aluminum straps, struggling to navigate the narrow staircase. Suddenly he yelped and started to tumble forward. Thankfully, he caught himself, but the crate didn't fare as well. It crashed against the wall and came to rest drunkenly on the landing at the bottom.

"Oh gosh, are you okay?"

"Yeah, I'm fine. Darndest thing! I'd swear someone pushed me!" he muttered, trotting down the steps and throwing a cautious glance behind him.

"Well, I'm the only one here." Maddie laughed.

"Yeah, guess I just lost my balance. Sorry." He righted the crate and pulled it back off the landing and into the living room. Then he deposited it against the wall next to the stairs in the spot Maddie indicated. It wasn't the ideal solution, but it would have to do. At least she could walk around it until she could unpack it and take the paintings upstairs one at a time. He'd hurried out the door, after thanking her profusely for the tip, when Maddie noticed the crate appeared damaged.

"Hey, wait a sec," she called out to the uniform-clad kid who'd already made it halfway down the walk. He hustled back onto the porch and stood poised in the doorway.

"'S up?"

"This is damaged." She pointed to the offending corner. She pulled away the strapping and saw that not only a frame, but one corner of a canvas was crushed. "I insured these. Do I have to fill out a form or something?"

"Oh." His face fell. "Yeah, sure."

"I'm sure it happened during shipping." She winked, and his expression brightened.

He pulled the pile of papers from his clipboard and rifled through them until he found the right form. He glanced at the label on the broken crate and scribbled in the information. Then he passed it to Maddie for her signature.

"How long will it take to get my money?" She handed the completed form back.

"Hard to say. Couple weeks, maybe?" He shrugged with disinterest.

"Swell." Maddie sighed. "Well, thanks again."

"No sweat. Have a good day." He nodded and headed back down the steps.

Maddie locked the door and then checked the limited amount of money left in her wallet. There were no two ways about it. She had to get to that mall Sam mentioned and find an ATM. Soon. But, before she did another thing, she needed to grab twenty winks.

The ringing phone thwarted her plan once again. Jeff Hagen wanted to show the house in thirty minutes. Seriously? The universe, it seemed, was conspiring against her. She plumped the pillows on the sofa and quickly ran into the kitchen to wash the few dishes she'd left in the sink that morning. She couldn't help noticing the smell of onions and garlic from her adventure in Italian cooking were permeating the entire downstairs. Probably wouldn't make for the best first impression on potential buyers. She tugged the small, plastic bag out of the wastebasket, tied the top closed, and headed out to the backyard to deposit it in the trash can. She made a mental note to ask Sam what day she should put out the trash for pick-up. Um, yeah, maybe not. She would ask Caroline.

When she finally got back to the sink, she stared in

confusion. The dishes she'd left in the sink were gone. Maybe she'd been so upset after Sam's defection and Ian's visit, she'd done them earlier and forgotten all about it? That must be it. Shaking her head at her continued inability to think straight on any matter concerning Sam Barstow, she left the kitchen and hiked the stairs to her bedroom to make the bed. She yanked everything into place, determined to treat it as just any other household chore and give no thought whatsoever to what had taken place between the sheets after they'd abandoned the sofa and headed upstairs the previous night.

She slowed at the top of the stairs when she noticed the door to her father's room stood open again. She briefly wondered if Sam had been in there for something that morning but discarded the idea when she remembered he'd already been downstairs when she woke up. The door had been tightly closed as she passed it on her way down, and Sam hadn't come back upstairs before storming out.

Heart thudding in her ears, she stepped across the threshold and flicked on the light. She shivered and rubbed her hands briskly up and down her bare arms at the noticeable temperature difference in the room. Okay, she thought, this is weird. It had to be at least ten degrees colder in this room than in the rest of the house, and that feeling she had company was back. Oddly, she didn't feel threatened, just vaguely uneasy.

"Okay, Dad," Maddie announced in a trembling voice. "If this is you, and you're trying to convince me to stay in Pine Grove, scaring the crap out of me is probably not the best way to achieve your goal."

She felt like an utter fool talking to the empty

room, but reconsidered the craziness of it when the light sputtered out and the room immediately returned to a temperature consistent with the rest of the house. Maddie shook her head and backed from the room leaving the door open. Probably nothing more than her wildly fluctuating emotions playing mind games. Yeah, that must be it.

Her heart tripped into double time when it occurred to her maybe the supernatural had absolutely nothing to do with the door being open. Maybe whoever had been in the house before had come back while she worked at Caroline's. Still standing outside her father's room, she yanked her cell phone from the back pocket of her jeans and scrolled through her contact list until she found Sam's number. She hesitated. He'd made his feelings clear. He didn't want a relationship, and even if he'd since had second thoughts, he had no problem jumping to the conclusion she was a liar and a cheat. She was on her own, nothing new. She swallowed hard and dialed 9-1-1, half wondering if she should be calling an exorcist instead. After providing the dispatcher with the information, she called Jeff Hagen back and told him they would have to postpone the showing. Then she went downstairs to wait for the police to arrive. Again.

****

Sam didn't enjoy his lunch at all. In fact, everything tasted like cardboard. He couldn't erase the picture of Maddie's exhausted face and accusing eyes from his mind. He'd called the garage as soon as she left to make sure Charley got the car done and delivered it today so she would have it at her disposal. Then he spent the next forty-five minutes avoiding the eye daggers Caroline threw at him while trying to tune out the none too quiet monologue she conducted under her breath about the failings of the Y chromosome, man-whores, and the overall blind stupidity of men in general. And Sam Barstow in particular.

He'd screwed up. Big time. After that first hard and fast tumble on the sofa, Sam had spent the rest of the night making slow, sweet love to Maddie. He'd intended it to be casual, but she touched him in places he'd locked away and forgotten. No matter how hard he'd been trying to convince himself otherwise, he knew she wasn't a wham-bam-thank-you kind of ma'am. But as soon as his own comfort zone was threatened, that's exactly the way he'd treated her. He'd crawled right back into his rabbit hole of defensive self-preservation and turned a deaf ear to anything she had to say. And then he left. After condemning her action for years, he'd done exactly the same thing she had. He simply walked out. God forbid, he should allow any woman to make a fool of him a second time. Then again, he'd managed to do a bang-up job of it all by himself.

Sam pushed his plate away with a sigh. He didn't know how to fix it. Maybe the best thing for both of them would be if he didn't even try. She would sell the house and go back to her life. And he would go on with his. That original plan seemed like a good one at the time. But that was before he'd been able to admit his preconceptions about Maddie were dead wrong. Before he let his defenses slip just enough to see she might be everything he'd always wanted and hadn't even known he was missing. Before his knee jerk reaction to Ian Sutherland's call.

Sam tossed a couple bills on the counter and tipped

the tail end of his milkshake into his mouth. Caroline wordlessly shoved the money in her apron, and started to clear the dishes away.

"How long are you planning to give me the silent treatment?" Sam asked with a lopsided grin.

"How long are you planning to be a buttknuckle?" she retorted sharply.

"Hey, wait a minute…" Sam began but Caroline cut him off.

"No, you wait a minute, Sam Barstow! I've known you for most of your life. I knew you when you were nothing but a teenage shit spending summers with your grandmother and bussing my tables for five bucks a day. I knew you when you were a big, hot-shot celebrity bodyguard everybody wanted a piece of. I knew you when you were falling down drunk and unable to get past the guilt about something that was never your fault to begin with. I also knew you when you picked yourself up and realized you were someone worth saving. Well, you know what, Sam? You're someone worth loving, too, but you never let any woman get close enough to try. How long are you going to judge every woman based on the actions of a two-faced materialistic bitch no one but your father ever thought was good enough for you in the first place?"

Sam realized his mouth was hanging open. He snapped it closed as Caroline swiped a damp rag angrily across the counter. Then he sucked in a long breath and blew it out slowly.

"Well, for your information, Maddie walked out on me long before Teresa ever did." He frowned. "Wow. You've been waiting to say that for a long time, huh?"

"I have no idea what you're talking about. I'm just pointing out that you and I go back a long way." Caroline turned her back to Sam, then opened the refrigerated case behind the counter and rearranged the desserts.

"Yeah?" Sam laughed. "Sure you were."

The older woman closed the door with a bang and turned back to Sam.

"Teresa was a long, tall glass of ice water, Sam— good for quenching your thirst, but tasteless. Common and available anywhere. In comparison? Maddie is...well, she's one of my chocolate shakes." She nodded her head emphatically, sending her earrings into a frenzied dance.

"Addictive, unforgettable, and worth the trip?" Sam cocked a brow.

"Yep," Caroline confirmed with another nod. "Hey, I like that. Maybe I should have it printed on the placemats or something. By the way, you might want to pull in a couple favors and see what you can find out about your father and an accident involving Frank Moran and a DUI shortly before Maddie left town. That and her coincidentally being awarded an art scholarship she doesn't remember applying for, about the same time."

"What are you saying, Caroline?" The world suddenly stood still and then tilted on its axis.

"I'm not saying anything at all, Sam Barstow." Caroline hefted her shoulders. "Just throwing a suggestion out there like a cookie. You have to decide if you're hungry enough to take a bite."

Sam slid from the stool and leaned over the counter to plant a kiss on Caroline's powdery cheek. It felt like crumpled tissue against his lips, and it surprised him to realize Caroline was no longer young. He'd never really noticed before. Caroline was…well, she just was.

"Thanks, Caroline. You're one of a kind, yourself. Anything else?"

"You're a big boy, Sam. You'll figure it out. Oh, and lock the door behind you. I'm closed for the day." Caroline snagged the dish bin and disappeared into the kitchen.

Sam pulled the door closed and jiggled the handle to make sure the lock engaged. He climbed into his truck and sat there staring into space. It shouldn't surprise him to discover his father's involvement in Maddie's disappearance ten years ago. In fact, if he was honest with himself, it wasn't the first time it occurred to him. Oh, not right away. Though he'd always known his father was a hard-ass, as a kid, he'd failed to grasp how ruthless the old man could be. Later, he'd wondered. But by then, it was too late. Years had passed. He'd moved on. He figured she had, too. On some level, it hurt less to blame a woman who professed to love him and walked away, than accept the reality his parent's pitiless determination for dominance took precedence over his son's happiness. But avoiding painful truth didn't change it. Though he tried to ignore it, the conviction he'd been wrong about Maddie insinuated itself into his heart almost from the moment she whacked some sense into his head with that lamp. Well, maybe Madigan wasn't willing to provide any answers about why she left, but he wasn't a heartsick kid anymore. He was a man who understood his father's true capabilities. He yanked his phone from his pocket.

Typically, the old man didn't waste time with pleasantries.

"It's about time. I called you two days ago," his father answered with a bark on the second ring.

"I'm well aware of that, but it isn't why I'm calling." Sam already clenched his jaw so tightly it ached. The man, even his voice alone, always had that effect. "I want you to tell me why Madigan Moran left town ten years ago."

"Who?" His father's response was immediate and no less arrogant, but Sam easily recognized the hint of caution that crept in.

"What did you do to her, Dad? What threats did you pull out of your little black bag to make her leave?"

"Threats? Don't be ridiculous, Samuel. You don't have to threaten people like her. You simply buy them."

"So you're telling me you paid Madigan to leave town?"

"I simply made her understand if she truly cared for you, she would set you free. Obviously, a girl like her couldn't offer you anything in the long run. She'd only ruin any plans you had for your life."

"What you really mean is she'd ruin any plans *you* had for my life, isn't that right? Because you know what, *Dad*? Maddie *was* my plan. And you know something else? Your attitude is an antiquated cliché. There's no right side or wrong side of the tracks around here. Pine Grove doesn't even have a railroad. The only divisions that exist in this town are in your closed little mind."

"Well," Edward Barstow sputtered for the first time Sam could remember. "She left, didn't she? And she wasn't even smart enough to take the money. Told me to shove it, in fact. Only thing she cared about was keeping her drunk old man out of jail. And I didn't have to arrange that scholarship. Hell, even I wouldn't send the girl out into the world with nothing. I'm not a complete bastard."

"Actually, you are," Sam ground out. She didn't take the money. She'd been eighteen years old, and Edward Barstow, the intimidating sonofabitch, made grown men quake in their boots. Yet she'd told him to shove his money. Her home life might have been a nightmare at times, but it was the only home she had. But, she walked away, alone and without a word to anyone. And he'd been so busy nursing his wounded pride he hadn't tried to find her and ask her why. And now he knew. She left because she'd believed sacrificing her own happiness protected the two people she loved most. Her father…and him.

"I did you a favor, son."

"You know what's sad? You actually believe that," Sam responded at last. "It doesn't matter who you hurt or how many lives you destroy, as long everything goes your way in the end."

"If she meant so damn much to you, why didn't you go after her? Admit it. It was nothing more than a youthful infatuation."

"I was a nineteen-year-old kid, and blind, naïve ass that I was, I blamed her. Of course, that was your plan all along, wasn't it? Well, guess what? I might still be an ass, but blind and naïve? Not so much. My idealism died a long time ago. You made damned sure of it. These days, my eyes are wide open where you're concerned."

"I saved you from yourself, Samuel. You should be

thanking me."

"Thanking you? No, I don't think so. Actually, I should be incredibly angry with you. In fact, I *want* to be incredibly angry with you. But honestly, at this point, I just can't get past the pity. I feel sorry for you, Dad. I really do."

Sam ended the connection before his father had a chance to formulate a response. His gut tightened into the same hard knot it always did after speaking to his father, but not for the usual reason. This time it had nothing to do with the disappointment of the all-powerful Edward Barstow in his eldest son. What sickened him now was the realization his father could be callous enough in his quest for power over his own flesh and blood to bully and blackmail a desperate and insecure eighteen-year-old girl to get it. Though Sam wouldn't have believed it possible, his opinion of his father sank even lower.

He needed to talk to Maddie. He couldn't undo the damage the Barstows had inflicted on her life, but he could apologize for his part in it. It probably wouldn't change anything, but he owed her that much. He steered the nose of his truck in the direction of the Moran place. And if she wouldn't open the door? Well, maybe he should swing by and make sure Charley had delivered the car. Yeah, right.

His pulse quickened, and his chest tightened as he turned the corner and saw the collection of black and whites parked in and around Maddie's driveway. He pulled into the curb with a screech, leapt from the truck, and hit the front steps almost before the engine stopped cranking.

Ignoring the yellow tape stretched across them, he

took the stairs in one leap and pushed open the front door without bothering to knock. He nearly tripped over a large wooden crate in the middle of the floor right inside the entrance. His loud curse brought Jim Delaney, closely followed by his K-9 partner, Elsa, flying out of the kitchen.

"Hey, Sam," Jim walked quickly toward him. "This is a crime scene. You can't be in here."

"What in the hell are you talking about, Jim? Where's Maddie? Is she okay?" Sam continued his forward motion as though Jim hadn't spoken. If anything had happened to her…

"She isn't hurt if that's what you mean. She's downtown being questioned." Jim flattened a hand against Sam's chest to stop him coming any further into the house.

"About what?" Sam demanded. He came to a halt but made no move to leave.

"Elsa got a hit on this crate of paintings. Looks like she's been dealing," Jim offered in an official sounding tone.

"Don't be ridiculous," Sam growled. "And what in the hell were you and Elsa doing here in the first place?"

"She called. Miss Moran did, I mean. She thought someone had been in the house again. She let us in to check things out, and Elsa got a hit on this crate. Found the goods hidden in a false back on one of the paintings. Look, Sam, you have to leave. I shouldn't even be telling you this." Jim swiveled his head around quickly to see if anyone had overheard, but everyone seemed to be busy elsewhere.

"Let me have a look," Sam muttered, stepping back

to where the crate sat.

"Sam…" Jim moved to block his way.

"Look, Jim, I realize this bust is a big deal to you, but it's a big deal to me, too. Maddie isn't responsible for this. Think about it. Why in the hell would she call the police and let a drug sniffing dog in her house if she had something to hide?" Sam crouched down next to the crate and committed the information on the shipping label to memory as his training kicked in and everything began to click into place.

"That's exactly what she said," Jim began uncertainly. "But what better cover, right?"

"Oh, for the love of…stop being such a Barney Fife," Sam muttered rising to his feet. "Has she been charged yet?"

"I don't know." Jim tugged at the brim of his cap. "C'mon, Sam, you have to leave, and if you tell anyone I told you anything, I'll deny it."

"Naturally," Sam replied, striding down the steps and away from the house. He failed to put two and two together ten years ago, and it cost him Maddie. He ignored his instincts six years ago, and it cost a kid his life and Sam his marriage and career. Hell, who was he kidding? Caroline hit the nail on the head about Teresa, and his fault lay in closing his eyes to the truth before he put the ring on her finger. The fact she and Edward were so attuned to one another should have been his first clue. But his instincts seemed to be working just fine at the moment, and he needed to swallow his doubts and pay attention. He'd need to call in a few favors, and right now, in his book, his father owed him big time. But first, before he did anything else, he had to make sure Maddie was okay.

He yanked his phone from his jeans as he jammed the truck into gear, and called Bill Jessup at home.

"Sam, you have no idea what this girl's life's been like for the last decade or so. Did it ever occur to you that maybe she's guilty?" Bill asked quietly.

"Nope," Sam replied confidently. He'd been burned. He'd spent years afraid to rely on his instincts and his gut. Well, they were both screaming at him at the moment, and he'd be an even bigger fool to ignore them. He'd told Maddie last night no one could change the past and the only thing you could do was move forward and try to do better. And hadn't he done a bang-up job following his own advice so far? He might not know how to atone for his father's actions, might not know how to fix things between him and Maddie, but this he could do for her. This he could fix. And then she'd be free to get back to her life and forget the Barstows even existed.

"Yeah." Bill laughed. "Me neither."

Chapter Twelve

Maddie slumped miserably on the hard, lumpy slab
that passed for a bed in the holding cell of the Pine
Grove Police Department. Her other amenities
consisted of a scratchy wool blanket, a small aluminum
sink with cold running water, and a stainless steel toilet.
Maddie planned to wait until her back teeth were
floating before she suffered the indignity of using the
thing right out there in the open. At least, given the low
crime rate in Pine Grove, she had the small consolation
of a private cell. Pale, green paint peeled from the
concrete block walls, and the strong disinfectant smell
tickled her nose and burned her eyes, but at least the
place was clean.

She'd been allowed the obligatory phone call,
which turned out to be a total bust. She needed a
lawyer, she needed to alert Caroline she wouldn't be in,
and she needed to make arrangements for Mr. Jinx to be
cared for. She only knew one person in town she could
count on to take care of all those things via a single
phone call. She'd swallowed her pride and dialed Sam's
number. He didn't even bother to answer. Maddie left a
message anyway hoping even if he had no longer had
any interest in her, he wouldn't want to see Caroline
left in the lurch, or poor Mr. Jinx starve to death. As for
a lawyer, Maddie supposed she was entitled to some
kind of court appointed public defender. Great. A total

stranger who wouldn't give a flying fig what happened to her, just like the rest of the world.

In the middle of her solitary pity party, a door opened and closed, and Maddie detected the sound of footsteps echoing in the corridor and heading in her direction. Sliding from the bunk, she moved toward the iron bars as Bill Jessup stepped into view on the other side. He placed his big, warm hand over Maddie's small, cold one where she white knuckled the bar.

"How're you doing?" Bill asked gently.

"I've been better." Maddie sighed. "Bill, I swear I have no idea where those drugs came from."

"I believe you, Maddie. Unfortunately, until we can get to the bottom of it, you're the scapegoat. They've set a bail hearing for later today, but the prosecutor will likely argue you're a flight risk since you don't actually live here." He didn't look her in the eye when he made that announcement.

"Swell. So, I guess this is home sweet home for the foreseeable future?"

"Well, yeah. Unless you're transferred to the women's correctional facility pending your trial."

Maddie felt the remaining color drain from her face. Prison. They would send her to prison. No one would believe in the innocence of a virtual stranger with no connections, little money, and a crate filled with drug packed paintings. She didn't have a leg to stand on. Maddie had felt alone in her life, but never more than now. She buried her face in her free hand as she started to tremble, a full body tremble that threatened to shake her apart. She would just disappear into the system, a sad footnote noticed by no one.

"Hey, hey, calm down. It won't come to that, I

promise," he added hurriedly, reaching through the bars to pat her on the shoulder, and squeezed his hand over hers. "Listen, Maddie. We'll figure this out. I promise. It'll be okay, hang in there."

"What other choice do I have?" Maddie whispered. Falling apart wouldn't help anything. She was innocent, and there had to be an explanation. She knuckled the moisture from her eyes. Between tears and lack of sleep, they felt as though they'd been worked over by a cheese grater.

"Listen, Bill," she began in a firmer voice. "I left a message for Sam, but I don't know if he got it. Could you tell Caroline what happened so she can cover my shifts, and let Hannah's daughter, Diane, know too? I was sort of cat sitting while Hannah is in the hospital. I'd really appreciate it."

Bill grinned. "You're locked up, and you're worried about Caroline's diner and Hannah's cat? You're too much, Maddie. Anyway, they already know. Sam took care of it."

"Oh, okay then." Her heart sank. Sam had gotten her message, but he hadn't come. Well, she hadn't expected him to, had she? "Tell him thanks."

"I will when I talk to him. He had to go out of town kind of suddenly," Bill continued with a smirk. "He figured you were safe in here until he got back."

"What?" Maddie simply stared.

"Well, yeah." Bill squirmed uncomfortably under her intense scrutiny. "Sam figured out the drugs are what your intruder broke in for. He figured you're safer in here if anyone decided to come back poking around."

"Oh he did, did he?" She hissed between clenched teeth. "And would he by any chance be the one who suggested to the prosecutor I might be a flight risk?"

"He expected you'd be pissed," Bill laughed. "He knows what he's doing, Maddie. Let him take care of it."

"At the risk of being redundant, I guess I don't have much choice, do I?"

"Well, not at the moment," Bill agreed unhelpfully. He turned his head to look back in the direction from which he'd come as Maddie heard a commotion down the corridor.

"I don't care what your silly rules say, James Martin Delaney. I've known you since you were spitting up on your mother's best dress, and I'm telling you I am going in there!"

"Sounds like breakfast has arrived," Bill grinned.

"Caroline?" Maddie whispered in surprise. Sure enough, Caroline came stomping down the hall carrying a large brown shopping bag. She'd traded in her mop of outrageous yellow hair for a shade that fell somewhere between neon orange and fuchsia, and almost perfectly matched the cowboy boots she'd donned over her green, leopard print leggings. Her eyes were heavily shadowed in two shades of purple, but the bright red lipstick extending at least a quarter inch beyond her lip line was still her usual shade and drawn artfully in place. She chomped on her ever-present wad of gum and kept right on chomping, even when her feet stopped moving as she waited for Jim Delaney to catch up.

"C'mon, Jimmy boy, I don't have all day. Hi, doll." She smiled brightly at Maddie while Officer Jim jiggled a ring of keys and finally fitted one in the lock, swinging the door open with a metallic creak. Caroline elbowed him out of her way and bustled across the cell to set the bag on the bed.

"Caroline, what are you doing here?" Maddie gasped in astonishment.

"Thought you might be hungry. A girl can't live by doughnuts alone." She paused to glare at Jim and Bill. "And nothing else in this place is fit to eat."

She began unpacking the bag and turned back to the two policemen, one grinning comically and the other looking decidedly nervous.

"Run along, boys. Just leave the door open, and I'll let myself out when I'm ready." Caroline waved them off.

"Caroline," Jim began in a pleading tone. "You know I can't do that. Are you trying to get me fired? She's a prisoner. I can't leave the door open!"

"Listen here, Hot Stuff, the only way out of here is right past your desk, so even if Maddie had a sudden urge to overpower me with a paper cup or a plastic fork, she's still got to get by you, right?"

"I guess so," Jim mumbled.

"I'll see you later, Maddie," Bill called, moving to follow Jim back out to the office area. "Hang in there. It'll be okay. I'll let you know if I hear from Sam."

"Thanks, Bill. I'll try."

Maddie sank down next to Caroline on the bunk watching in disbelief as the older woman opened a Styrofoam container filled with pancakes dripping in butter and maple syrup, and placed it in Maddie's lap. Her eyes filled and overflowed as Caroline continued to pull items from the bag. Coffee, orange juice, bacon done to the perfect crisp, and still warm blueberry muffins. And finally, a plastic package of serviceable cotton bikini underwear. At this stage of the game,

Maddie thought they might be an even more welcome sight than the food.

"I had to guess the size." Caroline winked.

"Caroline, I don't know what to say," Maddie sniffed.

"You aren't supposed to say anything. You're supposed to eat. This is what friends do." Caroline popped the lids off two cups of coffee and handed one to Maddie before taking a careful sip of the other. "Whatsa matter? You never had a friend, before? Knock it off, dry your eyes, and dig in."

"Well, I never had a friend who would bring me breakfast and clean undies in *jail*," Maddie mumbled around a mouthful of pancakes. "Who's watching the diner?"

"Decided I was overdue for a day off." The older woman smiled. The garish lipstick made her resemble a rabid clown, but Maddie discovered she'd developed a certain fondness for this particular circus. Maybe even enough to stay. Assuming she didn't have reservations in the penitentiary for the next ten to fifteen years.

Maddie continued to shovel the food into her mouth while Caroline quietly sipped her coffee. She wouldn't have believed she could be this hungry under the circumstances, but somehow the sight and smell of Caroline's food, Bill's encouraging visit, and the knowledge that Sam believed in her innocence and worked to prove it, made her feel marginally better. He might not want her, but at least he didn't believe she'd stooped to dealing drugs.

She swallowed a mouthful of coffee over the lump in her throat. She hadn't come to Pine Grove looking for anything, at least not consciously. But almost from the moment she arrived, she'd begun to feel like all the empty places in her soul were filling in one by one. And now she stood to lose everything, including her freedom. Her chest ached. It shouldn't hurt so much to lose something she'd never really had. This whole mess made no sense. She'd had those paintings framed herself at a new shop Ian had recommended. The guy had given her a great deal.

Maddie's eyes widened. She gasped, deftly aspirating a mouthful of bacon, as the epiphany struck. Caroline enthusiastically pounded her between the shoulder blades until Maddie held up a hand to stop her. Coughing until her eyes watered and her breath came in wheezing gulps, she suddenly realized who'd broken into her house, and why.

Chapter Thirteen

Sam dropped his duffel bag next to the sofa and tossed his keys on the kitchen counter, followed closely by his sunglasses and wallet. He snagged a bottle of root beer from the fridge and dropped his tired ass in a chair. Propping his feet on the corner of the table, he leaned back, and took a good, long swig while watching the sunlight dance on the rippling surface of the lake. His gut instinct had been right on the money. Ian Sutherland had danced with the devil to raise the capital to open his gallery. When he couldn't keep up with the payments, he'd been persuaded to front his benefactor's drug business, persuasion being a relative term. Sam learned the entire operation had been under surveillance for quite some time, but no one had been able to figure out how they were moving the product. He'd been more than happy to clue them in. Sutherland went on the run, but Sam figured the authorities, or his *friends,* were bound to track him down, eventually. Sam's features hardened as he thought of the way the bastard had used Maddie. He wouldn't mind being in on *that* takedown when it happened.

It had been galling to go to his father for help, especially after their most recent conversation; but what Edward Barstow lacked in empathy, he more than made up for in power and connections. Expecting to serve a mandatory stint in the corporate offices in exchange for

171

his father's help, he nearly swallowed his teeth when his father instead requested Sam design and oversee security for an important international business conference Edward hosted at the family's summer estate in the Hamptons. Sam dared to hope it was his father's way of admitting he might have been wrong. Not that Edward would ever concede it.

He'd been going nonstop for over two weeks, but it had been worth it. The meeting went off without a hitch, and Maddie was cleared completely within twenty-four hours of her arrest. Sam suspected he'd even managed to earn a modicum of his father's grudging respect. More importantly, his father's opinion aside, he'd proven to himself that he still had what it took.

Now Madigan had the freedom to sell her house and go back to her life, and Sam had the freedom to…what? He'd been perfectly content before she reappeared and knocked him upside the head, in more ways than one. There was no reason he couldn't be perfectly happy after she left. He breathed deeply, swallowed the last mouthful of soda, and relaxed into the familiar isolation of the lake house. It had been two weeks of kick-ass crazy and last-minute crises. The focus that had come so easily to him in his former life was something he hadn't been sure he was still capable of. Despite the lingering shadow of his epic failure—or maybe because of it—he felt pretty good about the battle he'd just won. And it was more than the battle to clear Maddie's name. It was a battle to prove something to himself. He'd walked away from his career because he doubted his instincts, doubted himself. Now he knew he could still get the job done. And apparently so did

Edward, who'd put an offer on the table that would allow Sam to be a part of the family empire on his own terms. Creating and managing a security division. He knew he'd be damned good at it. More than that, though he knew Edward would deny it until his dying breath, Sam thought maybe his old man grew as weary of butting heads as he did, and this was his attempt to meet him halfway. Because he'd seen Maddie struggling with the pain of things she couldn't change, he'd promised at least to consider it. Realistically, he doubted he could tolerate being a satellite in the vicinity of his father's gravitational pull. And the thing he did want? Well, he'd managed to push that away with both hands and a healthy dose of I'm-not-getting-screwed-again.

Sam climbed stiffly to his feet, leaving the empty bottle on the kitchen table. The only thing he wanted to think about right now was a hot shower and his bed. He staggered toward the bathroom, peeled away his flight wrinkled clothes, and let them litter the floor along the way. He reached into the shower and cranked the water on full blast. He stepped under the steaming spray and waited for it to loosen the knots in his muscles and wash his regrets down the drain. It was a hell of a lot easier to be happy with what you had when you didn't know what you were missing.

****

Maddie hefted the last box of clothes onto the tall stack already piled and waiting on the front porch with a heartfelt grunt. That did it. It had been a big job going through her father's things, in between working at Caroline's and getting settled in. After sorting through all the clothes, she'd decided to keep just one cardigan sweater and a plaid flannel robe that still smelled faintly of her father's pipe tobacco, and then packed all the other things for donation. Caroline had told her about Peyton House, a shelter for recovering alcoholics with nowhere else to go. Maddie called and discovered they'd be delighted to pick up the donation. Her father's things would find a new home with people who needed and appreciated them. People trying to turn their lives around. It seemed like a fitting resolution.

Aside from the clothing, she'd also found a stack of shoeboxes in the back of Frank's closet. A quick shuffle showed her the boxes were filled with photographs and memories, letters and birthday cards written but never sent, her mother's obituary, newspaper clippings from her high school play and every art showing she'd ever had. The boxes contained a collection of love and regrets, a life lost, a family sacrificed. Her father had never forgotten about her, never stopped loving her. Yes, he'd been flawed. But then, she had no claim to perfection herself. And they'd both suffered. None of it changed anything, but at least she'd been in his heart even if she hadn't been in his life. Just as he'd been in hers, as difficult as that truth had been to find. Once she got past the tears, she found it actually gave her some comfort.

In addition to converting the back bedroom into a studio, Maddie planned to turn her father's room into an office and guestroom. She knew she'd have to hire someone to move the furniture out before she could paint the walls and refinish the floor, but she decided she could clear the smaller things out herself. She packed the boxes of keepsakes into large plastic totes she'd purchased at the mall and carried them out to the garage. Once she had the house in order, she planned to bring them all back in and go through them again—maybe frame some of the photos, and put some of the cards and letters into a scrapbook.

Maddie had found it fairly easy to stay busy during the days, but she spent most nights tossing and turning, trying not to think about Sam. She'd swallowed her pride and called to thank him after she'd been released. He hadn't answered, nor had he called back. She thought he might at least stop by to fill her in on the details about how he'd managed to secure her freedom. But he hadn't. No one had seen him, and if they had, they hadn't mentioned it to Maddie. He'd even abandoned his usual habit of stopping by Caroline's for lunch. She didn't need to be hit over the head with a lamp to understand his message. It was probably just as well. Of course, now that she'd decided to stay, she would inevitably run into him sooner or later. Maybe if some time passed, it wouldn't hurt quite so much when she finally did. Maybe she could carry off casual. There was a first time for everything, right?

She just had come back into the house and finished washing the dust from her hands, when her phone rang. Drying them quickly on a paper towel, she grabbed the phone without checking the display.

"Hello?"

"Maddie? Hey, how are you? It's Jeff…Jeff Hagen. You never called to reschedule that showing, and I've got a couple who are anxious to see the place."

"Yeah, about that…" Maddie began slowly. "I've been meaning to call you. I'm going to be taking the house off the market for the time being. My roommate decided to move back home with her parents. So, I guess I'm going to be staying in Pine Grove for a while."

"I see."

"I know I should have called you right away," Maddie hurried to add. "But I've been kind of busy. Is it going to be a problem? I mean, I realize I signed a contract and everything…"

"No, no, it's cool. Stuff happens, right? Leave the sign on the side of the garage, and I'll stop by for it the next time I'm in the area."

"Thanks for understanding." Maddie smiled in relief. The real reason she hadn't called Jeff before this was the concern he might give her a hard time. She was still reeling over the fact Chris had been so shaken by the break-in, she'd decided to just up and leave without warning. Fortunately, Chris' parents had been so thrilled she'd decided to move back home, they paid off the lease and were even willing to foot the bill to pack and ship all Maddie's things to Pine Grove. Not that she had much besides her clothes, paintings, and art supplies to worry about. She had all the furniture she needed right here. She expected the delivery any day. Thank God, she'd had the house to fall back on. Turned out her father's plan to provide her with security had worked out exactly the way he'd hoped. Go figure.

"Just remember my number if you change your mind." Jeff laughed. "Hey, as long as you're staying in town, maybe you'd like to grab a bite to eat or see a movie sometime?"

"Oh, um, I'm kind of swamped with getting settled in," Maddie evaded. "Can I get back to you on that?"

"Oh…yeah, sure." Jeff's baffled tone revealed he fully expected her to pounce on the golden opportunity—a date with him, the most successful Realtor in three counties. Given his looks, his flash, and his fat wallet, Maddie bet he wasn't used to being turned down. Oh well, he wasn't her type.

Her type had broad shoulders and a heavily muscled chest, a narrow waist, a flat stomach, and slim hips. He had strong thighs, long legs, and wore steel-toed work boots. He had a smile that melted her bones and the bluest eyes she'd ever seen, killer dimples and a kind heart. And…he made her laugh. She'd wrestled with the fact he'd once had a drinking problem, but as she met more of her father's friends and learned more about his sobriety and the way he'd been able to build a new life, the fear became manageable. Not that it mattered. Sam wasn't the least bit interested in taking her out for dinner and a movie. Or anything else for that matter.

She glanced at her watch and made quick work of getting off the phone. Shoot! She was going to be late. She ran outside, pulled the sign out of the lawn, and set it against the side of the garage. She unlocked the garage door in case the movers came, and then hurried next door to check on Mr. Jinx. Hannah had been transferred to a rehab center, but if all went well, everyone expected she would be home the next week.

The cat regarded her from the back of the sofa with his usual impassive stare. He'd seen her every day for close to a month and never came any nearer than the length of the room. That suited Maddie just fine. She filled his food dish and gave him fresh water. Then she locked the door and hurried back to her place to grab her purse and laptop. Her portfolio was in transit with the rest of her things, so earlier she'd loaded the few paintings, the ones she'd been allowed to keep, into the car and would use the scans on her laptop if Ms. Sloan expressed an interest in seeing the others. If she wanted to make her appointment with the gallery owner before her shift at Caroline's, she was going to have to put the pedal to the metal. Arriving late would hardly start a hopefully profitable relationship off on the right foot.

"Wish me luck, Dad," she called out to the empty house as she left. She didn't *exactly* believe her father's ghost still resided in the house, but she no longer believed it was beyond the realm of possibility. Doors opened, items moved, lights and appliances turned themselves off and on at the strangest times. And once or twice, late at night, when she allowed the tears to fall, she swore she felt a warmth and presence, a sensation of someone gently stroking her hair. She'd gone as far as mentioning it to Caroline, the one person she knew wouldn't think she'd totally lost her mind. Completely enamored with the idea of Frank haunting the house, Caroline suggested bringing a medium friend of hers over to prove it. Maddie declined. Although she hadn't heard the voice again, the overhead footsteps, cool breezes, and scent of cherry tobacco in the air were frequent visitors, and somehow it was comforting to think her father remained there in spirit. She was half afraid Caroline's medium would prove he didn't.

She stopped to stick a note to the front door directing the movers to leave the boxes in the garage so they wouldn't get mixed up with the boxes on the porch in case they arrived while she was gone. Then she hopped in the car, backed out of the drive, and floored it in the direction of downtown.

****

Sam tipped back the last of his root beer and tossed the empty bottle in the trash bag with the remains of his lunch. Then he repacked the tackle box. He had nothing to show for his afternoon of sportsmanship, but he figured he'd probably fished the spot dry since it was pretty much the only thing he'd been doing for the last week besides listening to his beard grow. He had to go into town today, since he'd depleted his supply of nearly everything, well everything except a freezer filled with trout. He shouldn't have to worry about running into Madigan. He figured she'd be long gone. She had a life elsewhere, and Sam Barstow sure as hell hadn't given her any reason to stay. He hadn't been looking for a relationship, right? Yeah, well, he'd done a damn fine job making sure he hadn't found one, hadn't he?

When Sutherland had shown up right after he and Maddie spent that incredible night together, Sam instinctively reverted to defense mode, and he sure as hell couldn't unring the bell. Much better to sit out here with his ass glued to a dock than to take a chance on running into her and seeing that expression on her face again. The one that said she'd been willing to trust him in spite of all her shit, in spite of all his. And what had he done with that gift? He ignored the fact he'd never experienced the instant connection he felt with her with anyone since the day she left. He discounted the feeling of being exactly where he belonged whenever he was anywhere near her. He told himself it was casual, jumped her bones, and threw her trust right back in her face the moment she threatened his pride. Well, wasn't that fuckin' special?

Sam stacked the poles in the corner of the shed,

dropped the tackle box inside the door, and headed to the cottage where he took a minute to run a washcloth over his face and neck. He hadn't bothered to shave in over a week and probably looked like hell—and smelled worse—but screw it. He only planned to run into town for a few groceries. It wasn't like he had anyone to impress. That ship had already sailed. The only woman who'd ever really been able to touch his heart had been on it.

Chapter Fourteen

Silently calling himself every kind of a fool, Sam hit the blinker and turned onto Maddie's street. Part of him wanted to see if the place had actually sold, but the other part felt like he needed to punish himself for being a complete and total ass who'd let a good thing slip right through his fingers. He rolled into a parking spot along the curb on the opposite side of the street and shifted the truck into park.

Both the Realtor's sign and Frank's car were gone. Piles of boxes littered the front porch and a moving van occupied the drive, backed up to the open door of the garage. Sam swallowed hard. He guessed he had his answer. Maddie had moved on. Why wouldn't she? She'd told him herself there was nothing for her in Pine Grove. And if there had been even the smallest chance Sam Barstow could have changed her mind, he'd managed to blow that opportunity right out of the water. He should have returned her call weeks ago, but he didn't want to know she'd called him solely from a sense of obligation.

Well, there didn't seem to be any point in sitting here staring at the house as though Maddie would magically appear. She was gone. He shifted the car into drive and eased out of the parking spot. Maybe he'd stop at Caroline's for lunch before he went to the market. He felt like he could use a friend. Of course, he'd probably have to listen to her read him the riot act first, but he deserved it. Anyway, recriminations would be easier to swallow with a grilled cheese and bacon with tomato on french toast and fries with beef gravy on the side. Then he could wash down the entire lecture and an ocean of regrets with a chocolate milkshake. It might not make him feel much better, but what the hell, he doubted it could make him feel any worse.

He maneuvered into a parking spot across the street and had just climbed out of the truck and started toward the diner when his phone vibrated in his back pocket. He yanked it free and checked the display.

"Curtis?"

"Uh, hey Sam. Sorry to bother you, man…but, well…" Curtis hesitated and Sam knew exactly what his reluctant tone forebode.

"Where are you, Curtis?" Sam asked calmly.

"Kildare's," Curtis whispered in a shaky voice.

"You did the right thing to call me, kid. Just sit tight and hang on. I'm on my way."

Instead of crossing the street to the diner, Sam shoved his phone back in his pocket and did an about face. Lunch and lectures would have to wait. Praying he could get there before the kid picked up the glass, Sam strode quickly along the sidewalk. Fortunately, the Irish pub where Curtis currently waged the battle to remain sober was only three doors down.

****

Maddie was having her best day in weeks. Laura Sloane, the owner of the Four Square Gallery, had expressed an interest in taking three of Maddie's paintings on consignment and wanted to see at least four more of the ones due to arrive via moving van. The diner was crowded for lunch, but not exhaustingly so, and time passed quickly as Caroline spent the afternoon bragging to anyone who would listen about Madigan Moran, the famous artist, residing right here in their own little town. After about the fifth table, Maddie stopped trying to correct the misrepresentation and simply shook her head at the customers behind Caroline's back with a smile and a wink.

She'd finally met Bill Jessup's wife when the couple stopped in for coffee and pie. Just as sweet and friendly as her husband, Maddie hoped she and Claire could get to know one another better. A little bubble of hope percolated when Bill casually mentioned Sam had taken on a short-term security job to repay a favor he'd used to clear Maddie's name. Maybe that's why he hadn't been able to return her call? The bubble burst when Bill went on to say Sam had been home for over a week. Oh well, she'd pretty much accepted he wasn't interested, so she decided not to let the disappointment ruin her otherwise productive day.

When the last of the patrons paid their bill and headed out the door, Maddie told Caroline she would finish clearing and lock up. Caroline was battling a spring cold, and the cold was winning. Maddie realized exactly how much her friend had been pushing herself when she didn't even bother to argue, but simply sneezed her gratitude, sending her earrings swinging. Waving, she headed out the back door to climb the outside stairs to her apartment.

Maddie quickly scooted from table to table, wiping them down with bleach wipes. Her ponytail bobbed jauntily along to the tune she hummed in her head. She'd already driven to the mall a couple of times for some things for the house, and as soon as she finished closing the diner, she planned to make another excursion in the hopes of getting some art supplies until hers arrived. Since she had a local gallery interested, she needed to begin painting again. She swiped at the last table and grabbed a bin of dirty dishes from behind the lunch counter. She backed into the kitchen, pushing the door open with a hip, and loaded the contents of the bin into the nearly full industrial dishwasher. She turned it on, flicked off the kitchen lights, and made a beeline to the front door to lock it.

She reached to flip the sign on the door and froze in her tracks. Her heart stuttered, and then resumed beating with a painful thump. A flock of butterflies took flight in her stomach, congregating in a thick lump in her throat and making it nearly impossible to breathe. The man about to cross the street looked tired and scruffy, but heartbreakingly familiar in spite of the disheveled appearance. She rubbed her sweaty palms down the sides of her jeans and straightened her ponytail. Well, she'd expected to run into him eventually, right? She left the door unlocked and let her hand drop to her side, leaving the sign in place. She sincerely hoped all the pep talks she'd been giving herself about her ability to act casual had worked. Eventually had apparently arrived.

Maddie continued to stare, wondering what on Earth she would say, when Sam suddenly stopped and pulled his phone from his pocket. He spoke for a few minutes and then shoved his phone back into his jeans. He dropped his chin to his chest, ran a hand over the back of his neck, and then spun on his heel and stalked off down the street. Maddie stepped to the window and pressed her nose flat against the glass. She held her breath when the window began to fog, then stepped back with a gasp when Sam threw open the door to Kildare's Irish Pub and disappeared inside.

Her heart dropped into her sneakers. Her hands trembled. He'd walked away from his career, a career that had driven him to drink. Then he'd taken a case to pay back a favor he'd needed to gain Maddie her freedom, according to Bill. Her stomach twisted in a knot as the logical explanation for the scruffy beard and worn out appearance dawned on her. Sam Barstow was drinking, again…and all because he'd helped her.

Maddie flipped the sign and grabbed her purse from under the counter. She hurried out the door, locked it, and stashed her purse in the trunk of her car. Then she darted across the street and along the sidewalk in the direction of Kildare's. She didn't stop to wonder what she would say. She didn't even stop to wonder if she had the right to say anything at all. She only knew she had to convince him nothing justified going down this road. He'd beaten it before. He could do it again.

She pushed open the door to the pub, temporarily blinded by the transition from the bright sunlight outside to the dim interior. She stopped inside the entry for a moment to allow her eyes to adjust, then took a look around. A television, tuned to a channel clearly playing all sports all the time, blared from the far corner, and the forgotten smell of day old ashtrays and stale beer burned her nostrils, making Maddie wrinkle her nose. She first scanned the wooden booths, and then the stools lining the worn oak bar, until her eyes came to rest on a set of wide, familiar shoulders tautly stretching the limits of a dark blue T-shirt.

Maddie locked her shaky knees and squared her shoulders. Sam appeared to be deeply engrossed in an intense conversation with the young man on the stool next to him. Before she could work up the nerve to approach, the man pushed his drink away and slid from the stool. His eyes were reddened, and he appeared to be on the verge of tears as he extended a shaky hand to Sam, who took it in a firm grip. As the man walked toward the door, Sam turned to watch him go wearing a relieved expression. He froze in mid-turn as his gaze came to rest on Maddie. He slid from the stool and walked slowly in her direction, coming to a stop about three feet away.

"What are you doing here?" His voice sounded strained, his expression guarded, and Maddie couldn't help noticing he clenched his fists tightly at his sides. Maybe this had been a mistake, she thought. Taking a drink from a drunk couldn't really compare to taking candy from a baby, especially when bailing you out of your misfortune drove him to drink in the first place.

Maddie stiffened her spine. Helping her caused this. Even if he wanted nothing to do with her, she couldn't walk away and leave him to drown if she could help prevent it. If he hated her for it, so be it. She would rather live with that than see him fall back into a dark hole where he hated himself.

Maddie crossed her arms over her chest and lifted her chin to look him straight in the eye.

"Maybe the better question is, what are *you* doing here?" There. Maddie gave herself a mental pat on the back. That wasn't so bad. Her voice barely shook at all. He looked like absolute hell, and still it took all the willpower she possessed to hold herself back from throwing herself into his arms. "You look like shit."

Sam scrubbed a palm over the thick scruff adorning his jaw.

"Yeah, well, I just came into town for a couple things. Hadn't planned on running into anyone. Least of all you."

"A couple of things? Like what? A six-pack, a fifth of vodka? When's the last time you ate? I know how this goes. Believe me, I could write the book. You're better than this, Sam." Tears pricked the backs of Maddie's lids, and she lowered her gaze to hide them.

Sam's brows drew together, and his fists slowly uncurled. He took a step in her direction.

"What in the hell are you talking about?"

"I know about the security job. To repay the favor…to help me," she stuttered. "God, Sam, I would rather have spent a month in jail than see you like this. I'm here to tell you I'll help you in any way I can."

Sam took another step forward until he stood so close Maddie could feel the heat from his body. She wanted to wrap her arms around him and beg him to turn away from this course. She wanted to pull his head to hers and kiss him silly until he couldn't think of a drink, until he couldn't think of anything except her. Instead, she laced her fingers together and gripped her hands tightly in front of her, fighting the urge to touch him.

"And how exactly do you think you're going to help me? Congratulations on selling the house, by the way."

"I didn't…I mean, c'mon, this doesn't have to be awkward, Sam. I know what we had is in the past. I get that. But that doesn't mean we can't be friends, right?

This is a little hiccup, and I'll do whatever I can to help you. That's what friends do." She stepped closer, laying a hand on the hard plane of his chest hoping to convince him of her sincerity. Funny, he didn't smell like booze. He smelled like…fish? She wrinkled her nose. His eyes narrowed at her expression.

"Sorry, guess I'm a little ripe. I don't want to be your friend, Maddie."

"Oh! Uh…I just…I'm sorry." Maddie withdrew her hand as though she'd been burned, and stepped back. She blinked rapidly to hide how deeply his words cut. "What you do is none of my business. I shouldn't have come."

She spun on her heels and pushed through the door like the hounds of hell were snapping at her ankles. She raced across the street and jumped in her car. Out of the corner of her eye, she saw Sam exit the pub. She ignored him when he called her name and started in her direction. Blinded by tears, she prayed no other vehicles were coming as she threw the car into gear and screeched into the street without looking. A glance in the rearview mirror revealed Sam standing in the middle of the road with his hands on his hips wearing a puzzled expression as she tore off in the direction of home.

****

She hadn't left. The thought played over and over again in his mind like a broken record. Sam watched her go, wondering what in the hell had prompted her to follow him into Kildare's, and then take off the way she had. It hit him like a bolt of lightning. Maddie thought he was drinking again. And instead of looking the other way in fear or disgust, she'd followed him into the bar and offered to help. The corners of his mouth curled, and his heart expanded. Maybe that ship hadn't sailed, after all.

Chapter Fifteen

Maddie closed the door and leaned back against it. What had she been thinking? Of course, Sam wouldn't want her help. She'd helped quite enough by being the reason he'd taken on a security job in the first place. But the rejection of her friendship had hurt, really hurt. Maddie's stomach felt as though someone had kicked her in the gut. And as for her heart…well, she wasn't even going there. The lamp flicked on and then sputtered off though she was nowhere near it. She'd grown used to the occasional oddities in the house and didn't as much as blink.

She pushed away from the door and stepped into the living room to drop her purse on the sofa.

"Well, Dad," she sighed into the empty room. "I guess I'll never learn."

"Get out."

Maddie whirled, heart pounding. She hadn't heard the voice since that first time and had convinced herself she'd imagined it.

"Wha…?"

"You won't be here long enough to learn anything, bitch." There was nothing preternatural about *that* voice, and Maddie knew it well. Ian Sutherland stepped from behind the draperies and locked his fingers around her wrist in a painful grip. "You could have made this easier for everyone. You should have just given me the paintings like I asked. Now, where are they?"

Gone was the suave, urbane art gallery owner. Unkempt and wild-eyed, Ian Sutherland's features were twisted into a comical parody of the man Maddie knew. She barely recognized him.

"What are you doing here, Ian? Let go of me!"

She wrenched her body away from him in vain. His grip tightened and he dragged her toward the kitchen. The basement door stood open, and Maddie's gut tightened in fear. No one would hear her. No one would find her. Panic gave her strength, and with a final desperate jerk, she tore her arm free and sprinted for the front door.

Ian dashed after her, his progress slowed by the ottoman that shot out in front of him, striking him in the shins, and knocking him off balance. Maddie fumbled frantically with the deadbolt, glancing over her shoulder to see a thick gray shadow forming between her and the advancing threat.

"What the hell…" Ian waved his arms wildly in front of his face as the shadow enveloped him. "I can't see! Maddie, help me!"

"As if!" Maddie sobbed with relief as she yanked open the door and ran smack dab into a familiar broad chest. Sam's arms came around her to steady her and she clung to him as though she would never let him go.

Sam pulled away slightly and looked down into her face.

"What's wrong?"

"Ian…he…he…" Maddie stuttered. Sam picked her up and set her to the side, then strode into the house. Maddie stuck her head inside the door just in time to see the gray cloud dissipate when Sam's fist connected solidly with Ian's jaw, sending the intruder to the floor with a sickening thud.

"Call the police," Sam ordered over his shoulder.

"I'm starting to think they should set up a substation at my house," Maddie muttered in a shaky voice. She tugged her phone from her jeans and did as Sam directed while he disappeared into the kitchen. He returned moments later with a ball of heavy twine, which he used to secure Sutherland's hands behind his back. Maddie didn't question the restraint, but personally, she didn't think Ian looked like he'd be going anywhere anytime soon.

"Are you okay?" Sam straightened and turned to where Maddie stood trembling in the doorway.

"Yeah, I think so," she replied quietly. "Thank you."

"Don't thank me," Sam spat in a disgusted voice. "I should have seen this coming. This asshole never should have gotten anywhere near you. I can't believe I didn't…"

"Sam." Maddie stepped forward and pressed her fingers to his lips. "Here's how it works. I say thank you. You say you're welcome and let it go. He didn't hurt me, and he'll get what's coming to him."

The screech of tires interrupted whatever Sam had been about to say in response. Pine Grove's finest, Bill Jessup and Jim Delaney, followed closely by Elsa, pounded up the porch steps. They stopped in the doorway and saw Sam had already secured the suspect. Bill stepped forward and rolled Ian slightly to the side with his foot then let him roll back with little concern for the man's comfort.

"Seriously? Garden twine?" He smirked and turned

to Sam with a cocked brow.

"Worked, didn't it?"

Ian groaned and opened his eyes slowly. Then, he turned his head from one side to the other with wide eyes.

"Where is he?" he croaked.

"Who?"

"The...the old guy."

Sam stepped forward to stand over Ian's supine form.

"Shit, Bill. Guess I hit him harder than I thought." Sam grinned with absolutely no hint of remorse.

"Not you," Ian groaned irritably, struggling to rise to a sitting position. His eyes darted around the room, coming to a stop at the fireplace. Elsa began to whine and buried her snout in her paws. Ian visibly paled. "Him."

They all turned in the direction of his wide, fixed gaze. Maddie gasped and blinked hard to see through the tears that sprang up to blind her.

"Daddy?" she whispered in awe. Sam leapt forward and pulled her hard against him as her knees began to buckle. There by the mantel, in front of her painting, stood the figure who'd been its inspiration. Pale, serene, nearly transparent, but definitely and unbelievably Frank Moran.

"You can see me?" Frank smiled. "Well, it's about time. I've been trying to show myself for weeks. This being dead shit should come with an instruction manual."

"I knew it," she whispered. "I knew you were here. Oh, Dad, I'm so sorry..."

"You have nothing to be sorry for, baby. You were

a child forced to become the adult. What kind of father was I to let you walk away to protect me when I should have been the one doing the protecting?"

"You knew?" Maddie's mouth dropped open and he nodded.

"Yes, I knew. I'm not making excuses, but it's kind of like sticking your hand in a pot of boiling water. You do that...you get burned right away. But if it's cold water, slowly coming to a boil, the changes are so gradual you don't realize you've burned yourself, until the damage is done. I'm the one who lost sight of the important things. You and your mother paid the price. I was a fool, Maddie, but a fool who always loved you. Nothing could ever change that."

"I guess we're both a couple of fools. I should never have turned you away."

"You had every right and I understood. But you need to let it go, baby. Let *me* go. I don't ever want you to feel the slightest bit of guilt where I'm concerned. I want you to remember your strength is what saved us both."

"But..." Maddie pulled away from Sam and moved toward her father. Frank shook his head and started to fade, becoming so faint she could barely make out his features. "It's all right with me if you want to stay."

"No, it's time. I've been dodging the light for weeks. I had to know you'd be okay." He looked from her to Sam and back again. "I love you, Maddie, and I'll always be as close as the happiest memory you hold in your heart. In the end, they're the only ones worth keeping." Her father's voice echoed in the room as he glanced at her painting, smiled, and then disappeared from sight.

"I love you, Daddy," she whispered. Her throat ached, knowing it wasn't the tears obscuring the sight of her father anymore. He'd really gone.

For a moment, no one moved, no one spoke.

"Did you see that?" Jim finally squeaked in a voice two octaves too high. He cleared his throat and deepened his tone. "I mean, did you see that?"

Bill reached down to haul Ian to his feet.

"See what?" He winked at Maddie who gave him a watery smile in return.

"Frank! Frank Moran! Standing right over there!" Jim grabbed Elsa's leash and tried to lead her over to the fireplace. She tucked her tail between her legs and refused to move.

"Don't be ridiculous, Jim. Frank's been dead for months. You're working too many doubles, buddy. Or maybe that new baby is keeping you awake at night, huh?" Bill hustled his prisoner to the front door. "You okay, Maddie?"

"Yeah, I'm fine, Bill. In fact, I'm better than fine. Thanks for coming. *Again.*"

"Honest to God, I think I'm gonna recommend we set up a substation on your front porch," Bill chuckled.

"I just suggested that to Sam. Hopefully the next time I call you it will be for something as innocuous as an invitation to dinner." She grinned back.

"I'll hold you to that. Get the door, Jim." Bill jerked his head in the direction of the door, and Jim reluctantly followed without another word, dragging a still whimpering Elsa behind him.

Sam closed the door and turned to face her with widened eyes. "Did that really happen?"

Maddie released a shaky breath. "Yeah, I think it

did. Weird things have been happening ever since I got here, but I never mentioned it because I figured everyone would think I was crazy."

"I'll be damned." Sam scratched at his beard and smiled crookedly. "Leave it to Frank."

"Yeah, leave it to Frank." Maddie swallowed hard and cleared her throat. "Uh, Sam? Not that I'm not grateful for your impeccable timing, but what are you doing here? I think you made it pretty clear earlier you aren't interested in my friendship."

"Oh, you got that, did you?" Sam flashed his dimple and took a step closer. Maddie's heart somersaulted. She took a step back, but the wall brought her up short. He took another step, and she had to tilt her head back to meet his eyes. They were clear and blue, and crinkled at the corners as he reached for her and pulled her close.

"Well, you're right. I don't want your friendship. I want a helluva lot more. I love you, Maddie. I always have. I'm a blind fool, and I may not deserve it, but I want it all."

He dipped his head to capture her mouth with his, and Maddie clung to him with a desperation she didn't know she could feel. The familiar heat curled low in her belly and quickly spread. She melted against him for a moment, and then reality hit her like a bucket of ice water dashed over her head. She pushed hard against his chest with a strangled sob and turned her head away.

"I…I'm sorry, Sam. I meant it when I said I'd help you in any way I can. I swear, I will. But no matter how much I love you, I'm not my mother. I can't live that life again, always trying to look the other way, always

196

hoping things will change. Not even for you. I—"

"Madigan, look at me." Sam hooked a finger under her chin and tipped her face to his. He thumbed the moisture from the corner of her eye and locked his gaze on hers. "I understand those particular memory ghosts are potent ones, painful ones. But you are not your mother, and I am not your father. I. Am. Not. Drinking."

"But…" She narrowed her eyes and shook her head in confusion. "I saw you. You were in a bar."

"The guy who left right as you came in? He's only been sober for about three months. When I got there, he was sitting at the bar white knuckling a glass of bourbon. At least he had enough sense to call me before he gave in to the urge."

"You're his sponsor?" Maddie whispered in a choked voice as understanding dawned. Her relief nearly buckled her knees. "You really aren't drinking?"

"No, and I couldn't tell you the last time it even entered my mind. I promise, if it ever does, I *will* tell you. We'll deal with it together, and I won't hesitate to ask for help before the urge gets the better of me. The security job? I took that as much for my benefit as for yours. I needed to prove something to myself, and I did. And though it wasn't part of the plan, I think maybe I even proved something to the old man, too. End of story."

"But you said you didn't…" Maddie trailed off, wanting, no…needing to be reassured she'd heard him right. "You thought I…"

He gave a tentative tug and pulled her back against him when she didn't resist.

"Yeah, well I have it on good authority that

sometimes I'm a total ass." He grinned.

"Oh, I think we've established that, but it's not your fault. *I* have it on good authority it's an inherent abnormality located in some obscure gene on the Y chromosome." Maddie slowly smiled back. "That I think I can live with."

"I'll work on it."

She stretched up and pressed her lips to his before pulling away with a grimace. "But Sam…there's one other thing I don't think I *can* live with."

His brows knit together. "What?"

"That stench. You stink. Like dead fish."

Sam waggled his eyebrows in the most disconcerting manner and then tugged her in the direction of the front door. "I think it's time I showed you *my* place. I have this incredible shower…"

****

By the time they were spent and satisfied, they'd also used every last drop of hot water. Staggering together into Sam's room, he collapsed on the bed in a heap and pulled a shivering Maddie down beside him. She curled into him and in minutes, her even breathing told him she'd dozed off. He pulled his grandmother's handmade quilt over her shoulders and tucked it around her. She snuggled even closer, and Sam's heart expanded until it ached. He'd almost missed this. He'd almost let his fear and his pride close his heart to the happiness and hope having this woman in his arms had always provided. He pressed his lips to her damp hair, and she stirred, her warm breath fanning his neck.

"Sam?" she murmured in a groggy voice.

"Hmmm?"

"I never should have left without talking to you all

those years ago. I knew what your father was like, at least I knew what you told me about him. I should have seen through him. I'm so sorry. I should have—"

"Shhhh. I knew him better than you did. I should have realized what he was capable of doing. I should have come after you, or at least asked why you left. But we were a couple kids up against a rich, powerful bastard who intimidated the hell out of everyone. Yeah, we both made mistakes, but the blame lies squarely on him. Maybe it's time we leave the past where it belongs and concentrate on the present and the future. Besides, one good thing came out of you leaving."

"Really? What?"

"Losing you was Frank's a-ha moment, the impetus he needed to get sober and get his life back on track."

Tears pricked the back of her lids, and she lifted her head to read his expression. "Really? That's what he meant when he said I'd saved us both?"

"That's what he meant."

"Well, I guess that's a pretty good side effect, huh?"

"Yep."

"Thank you for telling me." Maybe sacrifice planted the seeds, maybe pain watered the soil, but something good grew out of that garden of heartache. Her father had regained his sobriety, his life, and his dignity, and she'd regained the father she loved. And Sam. Not a bad harvest. "Sam?"

"Yeah?"

"Were you thinking about going fishing again tomorrow?"

"If washing off the stink is gonna be this much fun,

I can go fishing every single day. Several times a day, in fact."

"In that case, I think you're going to need a bigger water heater." Maddie grinned sleepily and rolled over onto his chest. She propped her chin on her stacked hands and waggled her brows. "I may never be able to take a shower again without remembering how perfectly happy I am right at this moment."

"Future memory ghost?" he teased, raising his head to capture her lips.

"Definitely." She smiled against his mouth. "The very best kind."

A word about the author…

Sharon Saracino was born and raised in the beautiful anthracite coal region of Northeastern Pennsylvania. A lifelong love of writing took a back seat to real life while she got married, raised a family, went back to college, and finally decided what she wanted to be when she grew up!

Sharon is a member of Romance Writers of America, the Fantasy, Futuristic and Paranormal Chapter, and of the Maryland Romance Writers. When she is not reading, writing, or dabbling in photography and genealogy, she works full time as a Certified Registered Rehabilitation Nurse. She plans to win the lottery just as soon as she remembers to purchase a ticket; she also fantasizes about moving to Italy, brews limoncello, and spends time with her incredible husband, funny and talented son, and two crazy dogs.

http://sharonsaracino.com